GALACTIC STEEL

D.I. Brown

authorHOUSE®

AuthorHouse™
1663 Liberty Drive
Bloomington, IN 47403
www.authorhouse.com
Phone: 1 (800) 839-8640

Published by AuthorHouse 05/30/2020

ISBN: 978-1-7283-6312-7 (sc)
ISBN: 978-1-7283-6311-0 (e)

Library of Congress Control Number: 2020910105

Print information available on the last page.

Any people depicted in stock imagery provided by Getty Images are models, and such images are being used for illustrative purposes only. Certain stock imagery © Getty Images.

Cover credit for Claudio Coccoli

This book is printed on acid-free paper.

CHAPTER 1

JAPAN: THE LAND OF
THE RISING HELL

Japan, the "land of the rising sun" but for me, it's more like the "land of the rising hell". An engulfing, fiery hell that I want to desperately leave but I do not possess the required blueprint to escape it. You are probably thinking, "uh, okay…..what is your deal?" I will fully explain details…just work with me. My name is Kenji Jackson, a military brat who was living within foreign territory in Okinawa. Though I never lived in the United States, I feel like an outsider within the lands I was born in.

I am a mixture blend of two cultures of both American and Japanese. My father's name was Conway Jackson, a Major in the United States Air Force. He was a tall and muscular African-American man that stood at an impressive 6'5 and weighing 225 pounds. His Air Force Specialty Code was "11FX" or in plain English, a fighter pilot. Conway was a "Top Gun" that flew the F-16 and participated in a surplus of combat missions which were top secret. As a pilot for the Pacific, he was stationed in Okinawa, Japan. While serving in Okinawa, Conway truly embraced the Japanese culture. Conway possessed a passionate interest in learning the Japanese customs and traditions that he would frequently leave the Air Force base during after-duty hours to travel every inch of Japan.

While on military leave, he met my mother, Timokko Wu at a noodle restaurant called "Men Toguku" in downtown Kobe. My mother was petite but strong woman that was fiercely independent. She was a working as a waitress at Men Toguku and was serving her "future" husband dinner. Compelled and mystified by mother's beauty, my father was very eager to get her attention. His methods of wooing my mother over were by ordering a ridiculous number of noodles from the menu to stir conversation. He kept ordering bowls after bowls of noodles, so he could maintain a flirtatious conversation with her. Conway made Timokko laugh and she was captivated by his confidence and charm. The bill was over $100 dollars and his stomach were about to explode! My father told me it was worth the stomach aches and bloating because my mother gave him her phone number that night. My father and mother would contact each other for months and he would use his military leave for every opportunity to go see her. Conway Jackson was a romantic gentleman and proposed to Timokko on top of Mount Tenchi after a hiking excursion. Of course, my mother said "yes" and a couple years later, I was born at the Okinawa United States Air Force Base.

11 Years Earlier......

I must declare that the first ten years of my life were like the golden times. Japan was a fascinating place to live in my younger days. The sun was vastly bright that illuminated every square inch of land. I was living in the "land of the rising sun"; however, it was a different reality as a military brat. Though I lived in Japan, I was truly living the American lifestyle on the Air Force base. Every day, I wake up to the loud reveille in morning, hear the airmen marching and singing cadence, witnessed aircrafts flying and landing on the flight line, and listened the peaceful "taps" at night.

Elementary school was like any ordinary school in America. All of my classmates (who were military brats too) were American, the foods I ate were American (like burgers and hotdogs), and I watched American television. On my free time, I would hang out with my classmates and play football or basketball at the gym. It felt like I was living in an American bubble that I thought would never burst. The base was our "little America" on foreign lands.

During the summers, my father would be an annual participant in the air shows during the fourth of July. The excitement in my heart overwhelmed me when I saw my father performed daring stunts with the

F-16 fighter jet. My favorite stunt was the double barrel and my father would execute with ease. He was a maven of the skies, a magician of the air. I wanted to be a pilot just like my father because he was my real-life superhero. Our relationship was awfully close, and he would always create quality time for me despite his busy and unpredictable schedule. After his deployments, he would come back to me and take me out on fishing trips. Conway was a wise and patient man that always had the impeccable timing with words and actions. During a fishing trip, I became impatient and whiny.

"Fishing is so boring. They aren't biting." I said.

"You have to be patient, son," Father said. "Patience is the key to contentment. Your fish is coming. Just watch and see."

Suddenly, a large skipjack tuna bit my fishing hook! The fish was huge and extraordinarily powerful that I almost fell off the boat. My dad catches before I went overboard and he helped reel the mini- Moby Dick.

"See, son you did it." Father said. "Sometimes good things come to those who wait. Now, we can make some tuna sandwiches, sushi, or whatever you desire."

Those were precious times because he always told me life lessons or funny stories during his deployments. One good comical story was when my father pranked his best friend Captain Fredrick Derkins by switching his combat boots with cowboy boots in his locker. The amount of laughter that I had with my father could last generations. I absolutely loved him and wanted to emulate him as a man.

Most of my life was close to perfection except the times when I adventured off base with my parents to visit my Japanese side of the family. My mother's family lives in rural area of Makkari where there are acres of green land. As we travel through the farms in my father's sedan, I stare at the window dreading in trepidation towards our destination which was Grandpa's house. In my lifetime, I have never met a meaner, angrier, and bitter person like my grandfather. His name was Yu Lin, and he was a proud and prideful man. Grandpa continually boasted about his relations with a samurai nobility family during the Sengoku period. Every time I visit Grandpa's house, he was wearing his traditional black Kimono with scandals and carried his razor sharpened Katina. The Katina was passed down from multiple generations once used in many Japanese military campaigns. His convictions were very stout when it came to honor, family, and the Japanese traditions. He was a meticulous farmer that embraced the simplicity of life. My grandmother, Aiya Lin deceased before I was born which may be the catalyst towards Grandpa's misery or perhaps he was always miserable.

When Grandpa discovered out that my mother engaged to my father, he was vehemently displeased. He cried for months after learning about the marriage and held his grudge deep into his soul. Grandpa despised the American culture and resented me because I was not 100% Japanese pure blood. My father conducted many attempts to win my Grandpa's approval by working on his farm, buying gifts such as historic Japanese paintings and artifacts, and treating him out to dinners including large quantities of Sake. Unfortunately, no volume of kindness and generosity could ever impress Grandpa. If tenacity was a personified, Grandpa was the living and breathing model.

What made matters worse was the language barrier. Sadly, I developed a learning disability in speech which prevented me from becoming bilingual. No matter hard I tried, I could not comprehend the Japanese dialect. Predictably, Grandpa was highly disappointed towards my mother that I could not grasp Japanese and thinks I am brainwashed from western ideals. Grandpa emphatically loved his country and culture but did not accept the western influence from my father. Oddly, Grandpa never spoke to me except grunts. Every time I said "hello, Grandpa" he would just go "ugh" to me. Grandpa was definitely a strange dude.

The sun was setting by the time we arrived at my Grandpa's house and I took a deep breath before exiting the car. I asked my father

"Do we really have to go to inside? I don't like it here."

"Son, it's out of your respect of your mother. Please get out the car." He firmly replied.

Later that night, I remembered vividly at the dinner table was scolding my mother with passion and ferocious nature. I did not understand what my grandfather was saying but I felt his discern and dissatisfaction vibe. Grandpa was prone to glare at me with repugnance and never exhibited love towards me. While berating my mother, he kept glancing at me which I figured out that the argument was about me. My mother was just sitting there and absorbing each word that Grandpa spewed. Each venomous word that Grandpa utter only increased' my father's temper. Like Father, like son, my temper rose as well as I sat there silently. I had a serious axe to grind for my grandfather. I cannot fathom why he hated me so much. Maybe, it was because I was American, or because I was biracial. Perhaps, I was the product of a marriage that my Grandpa did not favor. Basically, I was the symbol of displeasure in my Grandpa's eyes. Out of nowhere, Grandpa pointed his finger at me, and my father rose from the table.

"Don't you point your finger at my son! Timokko, we are leaving!" yelled Dad. "You will never see my son or your daughter again! I am tired of this deliberate disrespect that you cast upon my family! Let's go!"

We left Grandpa's house immediately and hopped in the sedan. I heard my mother sobbing and whimpering. My mother realized that she will never receive honor from her father. Honor is a very sacred in Japanese culture especially the father/daughter relationship. During the ride back to the Okinawa Air Force Base, my father grabbed my mother's hand and ranted.

"I love you Timokko and I know you love your father profoundly, but I will not allow him to treat my wife like filth. I don't want Kenji around him. I asked for his blessings for marriage and he said, 'I don't want your black hands on my daughter'. We will never return to that house again!" My father honored those words and we never returned to my grandfather's house again, but those words were only temporarily.

When I turned eleven, it was the genesis of my dark hole of gloom. It was Fourth of July and just like every year, we had an air show. The sun was shining the skies and the temperature was warm and soothing. The air show was open for the public and the Japanese natives enjoyed the soaring planes tumbling and performing uncanny tricks. I was enjoying a hotdog with extra mustard and ketchup anticipating my father's F-16 fighter jet. I see my father walking on the flight line with his green flight suit with his 484th Fighter Squadron patches that had two lions as a design. Right away, I became consumed with ecstasy and yelled at my father.

"Dad! Dad!" I yelled with excitement.

My father marched over with his Hollywood-styled sunglasses.

"Kenji! What's up kid?" he said with enthusiasm "Are you ready for this incredible show?"

"Do the double barrel rolls when you're in the sky! And a couple of tumbles!"

"I can do those moves with my eyes close and steer the plane with my feet! I gotcha buddy" he replied. "Hey, I have a present for you."

"Really? What is it?" pleasantly surprised.

"Close your eyes, it's something awesome." He said. I felt a cold metal chain around my neck and chest.

"A necklace?" I said with curiosity.

The necklace glittered from the sun rays and had a medallion hung below. The medallion had a strange symbol with three diamonds which formed a triangle. The shape of the medallion was a grotesque-shaped hexagon that was cumbersome and unusual. I was puzzled and confused.

"Where did you get this necklace from, a different planet? How much was it, looks so pricy." I asked.

My father chuckled, "Son, this necklace is incredibly special. It may protect you one day when the time is right. I want to give this to you because it belonged to my father. It's a family abloom."

"A family abloom?" I questioned.

"Yes, I will explain to you when the time is right." He said.

"Hey Conway, it is show time! Get inside your plane!" hollered Captain Derkins.

"Okay, buddy I got to go. I love you kid." He said.

My father hurdled inside the F-16 and turned on the afterburners which roared like lions. He gives me the Air Force salute to me and takes off into the blue horizon. As my father was gliding into the ole' blue yonder, I retrospect about Conway Jackson. He was a mysterious man, almost a myth in many aspects. Throughout my whole life, I never met his parents, siblings, or any family members on his side. He never explained his origins of where he came from or elaborated his upbringings. The moment he gave me the necklace, an epiphany arose. "His father gave it to him?" I was very naïve when I was a kid and I should have asked more questions about his family tree. Heck, I did not have any aunts, uncles, or cousins on his side! I hear the crowd cheering which brought me back to focus on the air show.

As I stared up into the sky, my father conducted the double barrel roll as I requested with ease. The crowd was cheering with bliss and hooted.

"Wow! Time for the tumble!" I said.

My father does a loop before performing his signature tumble. He looped in Mach one speed and hovered in my direction. As I anticipate the tumble, a purple beam from the skies hit my father's F-16! The crowd started screaming in fright and chaos manifested. The plane exploded right above me, and aircraft fragments and balls of fire began falling into my vicinity. I didn't know what to do. I just witnessed my father's death in the air and I just froze. The wing of the F-16 was about to crush me and suddenly, my necklace glowed! A force field shoved the wing at the last second before it was going to kill me. Firefighters, ambulance, and other first responders were everywhere. I kept some form of faith that my father hit the eject button to safety. I was running around the flight line hoping that my father was alive. Regretfully, part of me wished I never attempted to find my father. Abruptly, I became traumatized when I perceived his lifeless body which was about a football field away. He was not moving and there wasn't a parachute. I attempted to run over to see him, but Captain Derkins stopped me.

"Don't look Kenji, don't look." Captain Derkins said with concern.

Captain gave me a comforting hug and I cried my heart out. I didn't know how I survived that dreadful day, but I didn't care, my hero doesn't walk on earth anymore.

The next morning, a military funeral was conducted. Hundreds of people were present from all five branches of service including the President of the United States. It was a murky and gloomy afternoon with enormous raindrops tumbling from the dark skies. Though it there was a significant downpour, it was a pale in comparison to the tears that was trickling down my face. Numbness engulfed me, and time sat still. The sadness and grief transported me into a different realm in which I didn't even hear the Chaplain's opening sermon or the Lone Bugle play "Taps". It was until the Marines conducted the honorary "21 Gun Salute" that startled me back to reality. The coffin was draped with the American flag. The Honor Guard marched over towards the coffin to conduct the traditional flag fold and presented the flag to my mother. I held my mother's hand trying to give her solace as the coffin dropped six feet under. Flowers were thrown in many directions as Major Conway Jackson was relived from duty.

After a month-long investigation of the plane crash, General Charles Williams invited my mother to his office. First, he gave his condolence to her and appreciated what Major Conway Jackson has done for his base and country. Then, he told my mother that it was mechanical failure that the plane crash and gave her a memo of the investigation for record. When she came home to tell me the news of what happened, I denied the claims.

"Mom, that's not what, happened! They are lying!" I yelled.

"Honey, it was an accident." She said. "I know it's difficult to handle this whole ordeal. Believe me, my heart is broken, and I still wish he were here. However, I believe in the General's investigation and facts. I know you miss him, and I miss him too, but bad things happen, Kenji. The engine created a spark which destroyed the plane. On the memo, it explains thoroughly of the mechanical failure."

"Mom, I am telling you! I was there! I saw this purple beam destroying the plane."

"Kenji, you are speaking non-sense. I do not want to hear anymore fabrication There is a video showing no purple beam in the area. Honey, it was an unfortunate event. Kenji, your father will always be in your heart."

"Mom, I am not crazy. The beam came from the sky like a laser and hit the plane directly. The plane almost landed on me and a force field protected me. And then…"

"Kenji! I know you are mourning, and you are trying to make sense of all this but you're in denial. I want to believe my love, my husband will walk through that door and say 'hey babe, I am home' one more time. But I came to realization that he is out of my life. That door will open, but Conway will not be there. I am sorry love, he's gone."

"I am not in denial! I know what I saw!"

"Hush! No more! Be quiet… I am sorry, I didn't mean to yell at you, but I am hurting too."

I did not continue my case about the purple beam with my mother because she doesn't believe me, but I don't blame her. A purple beam that hailed from the sky during a sunny day can be considered farfetched, but I know what I saw.

What made matters worse was that the Air Force evicted us off the base. General Williams said that we could stay on base for a year but after that, we can no longer stay due to policy. The Okinawa Air Force Base was my home for eleven years and now, it is being taken away from me. My mother and I had nowhere to go so she decided that we needed to move back with her father, my Grandpa! Ugh! My mother and I traveled to Grandpa's house. Once we arrived, Grandpa was standing at his front porch and stared at me. With no emotions in his face, Grandpa said, "You will meet in the morning at four to do work in the fields and feed the chickens".

I was shocked! I never knew he spoke English, and this is the first time I ever heard him spoke to me! Remember I said Japan is the "land of the rising hell"? You can call Grandpa's house, "Daunte's Inferno".

As I was unpacking and settling in my new dungeon, I saw my necklace that my father gave me. Memories started to project in my mind of the good times with my dad. I tear up for a moment and stashed the necklace in my closet.

CHAPTER 2

JEN HIGH SCHOOL

Seven years later.…...present time.

RING! RING! RING! My alarm clock wakes me up at 4:30 and I wipe the crumbs from eyes. I don't know what is louder, my alarm clock or Grandpa howling from outside.

"Kenji, Kenji time to feed the chickens!" he said.

Grandpa says "feed the chickens" every damn morning like I am incompetent or something. My daily routine is this:

1) *Wake up 4:30 and feed the chickens*
2) *Water the carrot crops*
3) *Feed the pigs and horses*
4) *Water and gather rice*
5) *Get ready for school*

My mother used every cent of the life insurance from the Air Force to pay for my expensive private school tuition at Jen High School. There are a couple of issues with this school. First, this school is far as hell! It sucks already that I must wake up at 4:30 every day to do two hours of hard manual labor. What make matters worse is that the school is two hours away which gives me a little time to shower up. Sometimes, I say, *"fuck it"* and go without a shower and fresh up once I get to the school gym. There are multiple mountains and steep hills that I must ride my bike through which is good cardio but tiring. It takes about forty-five minutes to find the bus stop and if I am late, then I am screwed. The bus picks me up and drops me off in a town called Tari and the school is about ten blocks away. Tari is a bizarre, busy, small city that isn't bicycle friendly. I ride my bike through unfinished paved sideways and heavy traffic. There's always a chance that I may hit by inconsiderate drivers who don't give a shit about pedestrians. I weave through like a basket and make it to Jen High just in time but soak and wet with sweat. I am the only person who rides their bike to school because everyone else is from wealth and privilege. While my main transportation is pedals and gears, most of the students at Jen High are driving fancy sports cars or stretched out limos with a chauffeur. I am the poorest student at Jen High and the least popular. Most of all, I stick out because I am only half-Japanese. I lock my bicycle on the rack and hit the gym for the showers, so I won't stink for class.

The first few years at Jen High School were a struggle. It was a culture shock with a thousand jolts. For starters, this school looks like a Buckingham Palace replica. You would think that the Queen will be knighting nobleman here. There is flowing water foundations splashing in the courtyard, groomed green bushes concisely cut, and sculpted statues of random people that I could care less about. Classical waltz music is constantly playing throughout the courtyard which enhances the snobby atmosphere. The buildings are juggernaut size with roman styled pillars and gigantic steps. I am telling you, the only thing that Jen High school needs are the soldiers with the fuzzy hats and call it England.

Being an American kid in a Japanese school is a demoralizing for me. This school is very advanced and teaches at an accelerated level. It isn't like a typical American school where you get the summers off. I am in school for over 200 days! The students at Jen High know English fluently and sound better than most Americans! However, the teachers taught only in Japanese and I didn't know squat due to my speech disability. I only know enough Japanese to get by and my mother is my official tutor. The students love to mock me when I spoke in class because of my accent. The ringleader of jokes is Tam Hideki, the biggest asshole ever. Tam is a tall, fat blob who could eat a ton of sushi in one sitting. His body odor is terrible with a stench breath to match. Tam is a perennial bully and his expertise is being a douchebag. This jerk tortured me since I joined this Japanese school. It's senior year and he continues his bully campaigns. Every day, Tam always calls me "hafu" which means half-Japanese and punches me right in stomach for no reason right before class. Everyone laughs and giggles while my stomach is in agony. I walk inside the lecture hall and class is in session. My history teacher, Mr. Zaki is going around the class handing out permission slips for an upcoming field trip at Mount Tenchi. It's an historic site where the legendary story of a Samurai mysteriously fell from the skies and saved a village from two dragons. As class is ending, I get hit with Tam's spitball.

"Hafu! Are you attending the field trip?" said Tam with a vicious grin.

"Yes, I will. Why?" I said as I wipe off the paper off my face.

"Because I will kick your ass on top of Mount Tenchi and love to see you tumble down. Hafu!"

Tam darts another spitball but this time, it hits my right ear. The class laughs hysterically and chants "Hafu, Hafu". I run out of class in humiliation and try to find my bike, so I can just go home. I check the bicycle rack that's in the front of the school, but it is missing!

"Looking for your bike, Hafu?" Tam said with sarcasm as he is standing right behind me.

I turn around. "Tam, what the hell did you do with my bike?" I said.

"It's over there; the street sweeper is going to crush it just about now." Tam said with a wicked laughter.

"No! You bastard!" I scream.

I try to stop the street sweeper, but it is too late. The street sweeper annihilates my bike into pieces. The only thing that survives are the handlebars. I am spilling with rage.

"You jerk! Why did you do that for?" I said with disgust.

"Hafu, you're the only person at Jen High who rides a bike to school which is pathetic! So, I did you a favor by destroying it. You can fit in now…... not! You don't look like us nor can you speak Japanese. It's embarrassing that you're half Japanese and don't know the language. I am fluent in five languages which are Spanish, English, Latin, French, and most importantly Japanese! Yet, you can't grasp Japanese at all. Do yourself a favor and go back to America, you disgrace! I don't know how you will make it to school tomorrow since you're a broke-ass kid that lives on a farm. Maybe, you can use your horses to get to Jen. Ha-ha!"

The students in my class were outside joining the degradation ceremony by forming a circle, pointing their fingers, and chanting "Hafu". This is my boiling point. I didn't care if I get my ass kicked, I am fighting back. For seven hellish years, this blob keeps embarrassing me, but I had enough of his antics.

"Fuck you!" I scream which shocks Tam.

Rage is building, and my fist is clenching. I throw a haymaker to Tam's face and BAM! … he falls like a bowling pin. The students stops chanting "Hafu" and becomes silent. Tam gets up gingerly with blood dripping down his chin.

"You're going to die!" Tam yells.

"That's enough boys! In my office, right now!" hollers Principal Wong.

Tam and I are standing in Principal Wong's office waiting for our punishment. Tam is staring at me smiling with a smirk on his face because he knows that he won't get in trouble. Principal Wong's best friend is Tam's father, Jin Hideki who is the mayor of Tari and owns a plethora of sushi bars. Jin donates millions of yen towards Jen High School so the political corruption is repulsive. Tam didn't receive any reprimand or a slap on the wrist. Matter of fact, Principal Wong gives Tam a warm and friendly pat on the back!

"Tam, your father is a good man. His sushi restaurants are superb! I am stopping by for a visit tonight to discuss our endowment funding for the school. I will see you later, Tam. Stay out of trouble." Principal Wong utters.

"Ok, Principal Wong! See you later." said Tam as he leaves the Principal Wong's office.

As Tam walks away, he whispers "I will kill you at Mount Tenchi."

"Enjoy your busted lip, punk!" I said with sarcasm.

"You will be assigned extra homework and detention for a week!" yells Principal Wong.

"What? He destroyed my bike!" I protest.

"Bicycles are disposable items that can be easily replaced. You conducted violence at Jen High School which is against our traditions and moral ethic codes. Instead of utilizing words to mitigate the problem, you used your fists which are savage tactics. We are a prestigious educational institution and we don't need or require "rift raffs" sabotaging our flawless reputation.

I should expel you, but I won't due to my grace and minimal mercy that I still possess. Consider yourself warned."

"What? A rift raff? Listen, I may not be from wealth like the others, but I am not a piece of trash! That bicycle may be disposable to you and other folks that can afford it, but that's my only form of transportation. That Tam asshole destroyed it and you're letting him off the hook!"

"Two weeks of detention! Don't you defy me! That disgusting barbarian dialect is not permitted here. You barely pass your classes due to your language barrier. Tam Hideki is the valedictorian at Jen High who possesses scholarships from Harvard, Oxford, and all universities across Japan. It's a miracle that you're still enrolled here because you can barely sniff a scholarship. You harmed our generous donor, Mr. Jin Hideki's son which could potentially impact our endowment. I won't let anyone affect our thriving and admired school. Especially to someone like you who should be in full gratitude that we allowed someone of low caliber through our golden doors. I will remedy this incident with Mr. Hideki tonight over dinner with him. If you say something else, you will be expelled. Do you understand?"

"Yes, I understand. "I grunt.

"Get out of my office now before I find some other suitable punishment for your transgressions."

I leave Principal Wong's office with repulsion. With no bicycle, getting home is a journey. What was a 45-minute bike ride to the bus stop to Makkari is presently a two-hour march. What sucks even more is that I don't have any friends at this school. I feel alone in this world with no allies to call my own. My mother is the only thing I can consider as a friend, but she can't be there all the time due to her working nights at the local noodle restaurant. I pick up my book bag, inhale deeply, exhale like a dragon, and begin my long journey home.

As I am walking through downtown Tari and my feet are beginning to hurt. I am still pissed from the outcome of Principal Wong's punishment until I heard a sweet and angelic voice.

"Hey, Kenji!"

I turn around and there is a girl in a long, white stretch limo with her window down. "Who are you?"

"My name is Amaya Aiko. I am in your class. I sit up front usually, do you remember?"

Amaya is a gorgeous lady with long, jet black hair. It's amazing that I haven't notice her before. Maybe, it's because she is not wearing glasses. "Uh, I am sorry, I don't recall. What do you want?"

"Nothing, I just notice you don't have your bike and I saw what happened. Tam can be a jerk sometimes and I feel bad." Amaya said.

"Feeling bad or giving sympathy will not bring my bike back. I am trying to get home before dark. I have to go now." I said in despair.

"Wait, I can give you a lift. Where do you live?" Amaya asks.

"Makkari, it's extremely far from here. Thanks for the offer, but I have to say no." I said.

"It's only 45 minutes to your hometown by limo. I am planning to skip my time-consuming ballet lessons anyways. My driver Phillip will take me anywhere." Amaya said.

"That's okay, I can figure out a way," I said.

"Don't be so stubborn and prideful. Hop in silly!" Amaya said with determination.

I have never met anyone in my eighteen years of life that is so eager to take care of me. I took up her offer and enter her limo. The limo seats are soft leather, and the sweet aroma is like a flower garden.

"Phillip, take us to Makkari," said Amaya.

"Yes, madam." Phillip replies.

At first, there is an awkward pause in the first few miles, but Amaya starts speaking to me.

"So, you're half Japanese?" she asks.

"Yeah, can't you tell?" I reply with smugness.

"I apologize, did I offend? I am just breaking the ice."

"No, I am not offended. I just only wish that the Japanese people could accept me, but they see my skin hue and automatically have presumptions about me." I said.

"I don't have any presumptions, just simply curious about you. I heard that you are American." Amaya said with delight.

"Yes, I am American that's born in Japan on the Okinawa Air Force Base. My father was a fighter pilot and my mother from Japan. That's how I got the name Kenji." I said.

"Kenji is a great name. That's my grandfather's name; he is a retired sumo wrestler." Amaya said.

"Awesome." I said with a smirk.

"You don't talk much do you?" Amaya said with curiosity.

"Only if it's necessary." I said.

"This only means there's more discover about you, Kenji. Would you like to eat lunch with me on the field trip?"

"Uh…sure?" I said.

"Great! Well we are almost at your house, Kenji. It's a pleasure of meeting you and getting to know you somewhat better. We aren't strangers anymore."

"Thanks for the ride. But I have a question for you Amaya, why did you give me a ride in the first place? Why were you so compelled to help me?"

"I really don't know, Kenji. I feel vibes from people and many of those kids at Jen High aren't genuine. For some reason, I feel your spirit and my intuition followed it. Sorry, don't want to sound creepy or anything."

"No, it's not creepy. I appreciate that." I said.

"Well, here's your house. I will speak to you soon. Take care, Kenji. Here is my number."

Amaya grabs my phone and locks her digits into my contact list. I shake her hand and left her limo. Did an attractive lady just pick me up from Tari, drops me off at my house and gave me her number? This is a surreal moment on a dreadful day; however, my day ends on a high note. As I walk in my house, my Grandpa starts shouting at me.

"Kenji! What is wrong with you?" Grandpa yells with anger.

"What did I do?" I reply.

"What didn't you do? First, you forgot to feed all the chickens. Half of the coup is not fed. Second, there are no rice crops in the house. What do I tell you? Once you harvest the rice, bring it in the house! It's not that difficult, Kenji! Thirdly…"

Grandpa nit-picks me every day and after a while, I just tune him out. He continues his rhetoric, but I don't pay attention. After a while, I realize he barks more than he bites. However, he sees my bruised hand.

"Kenji! What is wrong with your hand?" Grandpa said with puzzlement.

"I fell down at school."

Grandpa with his quick reflexes slaps the back of my head!

"Boy, don't you lie to me. Now tell me again, what did you do with your hand?"

"Okay, Grandpa. I got into a fight with this bully named Tam. I punched him in the face because he wrecked my bike."

Oddly, my Grandpa became very calm and his whole demeanor changes.

"You were in a fight?"

"Yes, he tossed my bicycle in front of a street sweeper and now I have no bike. I became angry and punched him. I don't regret it!"

"Kenji, I am pleased that you defended yourself, however, you lost the battle."

"Huh? I punched him, and I won."

"No, no, you lost. I was acknowledged by your principal and he told me what happened. No matter what happened, you were the only one who was punished."

"Grandpa, Principal Wong's best friend is Tam's father. There's corruption at Jen High and I hate it. Tam gets away with everything and I get punished because I defended myself."

"Did Tam hit you first?"

"He wrecked my bike!"

"Did Tam hit you first?"

"No, I did but..."

"But nothing! You let him get under your skin and he won because you lost your temper. Tam rattled you to the point that you lost control. "He will win who knows how to handle both superior and inferior forces. If you knew that Tam Hideki is going to win no matter what, then you should have retreated. You must see the bigger picture instead of getting caught up with the paint strokes. You are there for your education, that's the picture. Though you hit Tam, who actually won? Did hitting him get your bike back? Now, you have detention for two weeks, extra homework and no bike. Tam is free. You didn't win, you lost."

"You might be right in theory, but you have to understand something. You don't know what it is like to be in my shoes. I am poorest student, and nothing compared to these spoiled rich kids. I am tortured by the mockery and forced to endure the pain. School is hell for me. I hate living here but I have no choice."

"You always have a choice. Today, you chose to fight which led to far more consequences. You don't fight with your fists but your mind. Speaking of mind, I do mind that you feed the chickens and get the rice crops into the house!"

"Yes, Grandpa..."

Grandpa lacks the comprehension my plight. Nonetheless, I do appreciate that he attempted to use his tutelage for the first time in my life, but I feel like it's too late. Should restraint violence because I know I will always lose? Should I get harsh torture every day no matter what happens? It doesn't make logical sense to me. I am sick of being a loser. I am sick of feeling poor. I am tired of being sick and tired. After feeding the chickens and storing the rice in the pantry, I take a good shower and head to my bedroom. I put my book bag in my closet and suddenly my necklace falls to floor. I have not seen this necklace in years and old memories start to project in my mind. I remember Tam threatening to kill me on Mount Tenchi, so I will bring my necklace for protection like the air show. I still believe the necklace saved my life from the F-16 crashing on me or maybe it is just a figment of my child imagination. I will wear the necklace for the trip just in case.

CHAPTER 3

MOUNT TENCHI

RING! RING! RING! The alarm disturbs my sleep and I am dreading this morning more than usual. I am bike-less and have no clue how I will go to school today. Grandpa will be pissed off at me, but I will skip doing the chores. With no bike, I have no choice but to walk through the steep hills and mountains. As I'm sneaking out the backdoor, Grandpa caught me red-handed.

"Hey Kenji! You didn't do your chores, what the hell!"

"Grandpa, I am sorry, but I can't do the chores this morning. I have no bike, plus a long walk to the bus stop and you and mom don't drive!"

"No excuses. You have responsibilities and you must fulfill them. Do not neglect our duties due to your predicaments. Feed the chickens now."

"Grandpa, I will miss the bus if I don't leave at this minute."

"Feed the chickens or no dinner!"

"What the hell?"

"You heard me, feed the chickens and don't you swear at me again. Mr. Wong is right; you do have a foul mouth."

"Fine! I will feed your goddamn chickens."

Angrily, I go to the chicken coup and feed the chickens. Then, I finish my other agricultural duties and report back to my Grandpa.

"It's all done sir. Can I go now? I will miss my bus!"

"Yes, you can Kenji. By the way, go to the back of the chicken coup, you have seeds everywhere. Sweep it."

"Grandpa! I have to go!"

"No dinner if you ignore my commands."

"Jesus Christ!"

Swiftly, I grab a broom from the closet and ran to the chicken coup. I rush there however, there are no seeds but a brand-new mountain bike.

"Holy crap! This bike is beautiful! Did you buy this Grandpa?"

"Hell no, but I did assemble it last night."

"Did mom buy it?"

"No, no, no it was your friend."

"Grandpa, I have no friends."

"I thought that pretty young gal that dropped you off last night was your friend. I am shocked that a girl would talk to you since you look hideous. Ha, ha, ha! Anyways, she gave you some brand-new wheels and I put it together for you."

"Wow! No one ever gave me a gift before since my father died. Thanks for assembling the bike Grandpa."

"I pitied you and out of my sympathy from your predicament, it was the least I could do. By the way, I must show you how to fight in combat."

"I knocked out that bully with one punch. I can hold my own don't you think?"

"No, that was a sucker punch. That bully will come back again for retaliation. After your school trip, I will show you the samurai ways."

"Samurai ways?"

"Yes, it's been passed down from generation to generation. It is an ancient tradition that I must bestow upon you. I was apprehensive to teach you because you are not full blood Japanese, but I am doing my family's legacy a disservice for not teaching the way of the samurai. After school, I will embrace you into the true Japanese customs. Now, go to school before you are tardy!"

"Wow, thanks Grandpa. I can't wait when you show me some moves and…"

"Get the hell out of here!"

"Yes, sir!"

I hop on my new mountain bicycle and it is *pretty* sweet. The paint is jet black with gold stripes with my name stitched in cursive on the seat. It is an Ice Dragon brand, Japan's most famous bicycle which the price ranges from 100,000 to 200,000 yen! I can't believe that Amaya would spend that much cash on a poor kid like me.

I get to school barely on time and squeeze enough seconds for a quick shower at the gym. After freshening up, I walk down the hallway and see Amaya at her locker. I approach her and gave Amaya my full gratitude.

"Amaya, I can't believe you bought an Ice Dragon for me. That was nice of you, but I can't accept it."

"You are very welcome and don't be silly, keep the bike."

"I can't accept this bike, it's over 150,000 yen!"

"My father owns Ice Dragon; it didn't cost me a thing. Just keep it to humor me, okay."

"Your father owns Ice Dragon? Say what?"

"Yes, he is the CEO of Ice Dragon. He is never in town and always on business trips to expand the brand. My father is trying to tackle the European market and he's always in England or Belgium living through a suitcase. I barely see him, and it saddens me when he is not around."

"Sorry to hear that. At least you have a father. My old man died in front of my eyes."

"You said your father die?"

"Yeah, it was very dramatic and..."

RING! RING! The school bell interrupts the conversation.

"Tell me more on the bus for the field trip to Mount Tenchi. We must go to class now. See you later"

"See you later, Amaya."

Amaya is a tender soul. She breaks the stereotype of these rich snobs in this school. Does she genuinely like me? It's foreign territory for me. I never had a female approach me like this before and I am beginning to have some love at first sight feelings for her. It's strange yet I accept this feeling of adoration. Quietly, I walk into the classroom and Mr. Zaki is giving field trip instructions.

"Ok, my pupils." said Mr. Zaki. "There are some rules when we get to Mount Tenchi. Safety, safety, safety! Be careful on Mount Tenchi, it's extremely dangerous. Watch out for cliffs because of the altitudes are remarkably high. I don't want to report a dead pupil because he or she was clumsy and careless. Wear your seatbelts on the bus, no gum, no foul language during the tour, no...."

Purposely, I start to daydream from Mr. Zaki's boring field trip instructions by staring at the window. I couldn't get my mind off Amaya. She's an elegant and beautiful girl. I wonder if I can make her my girlfriend on this trip. Maybe, she will say yes but why would she want a poor kid that barely passes in this school? Amaya is incredibly special and rare. I must cease the opportunity on this trip.

"Hey, Kenji! Pay attention!" yells Mr. Zaki.

"Sorry, Mr. Zaki"

"Where was I? Oh, yes. Everyone stay close, I don't want to lose anyone on the trip. Ok pupils, hop on the charter bus!"

As I am boarding the charter bus, I see that Amaya sitting down and an open seat next to her. I feel like this is my chance to get more quality time with Amaya so I rush down the bus aisle to get to her. Unfortunately, by the time I got to Amaya, it was Tam sitting next to her. That bastard took away my opportunity to sit with her, so I had to sit in the back of the bus alone. Once again, I feel like a pariah of Jen High. While on the road, Tam periodically keeps looking at me with a menace grin on his face. Tam is trying to get my attention by throwing paper balls at me. One hits me square on the forehead.

"What the hell man!" I said.

"Open up the ball, Hafu."

I open the paper ball and it had a message. It said, "You will die on this trip. See you in hell."

The bone chilling message makes me instantly petrified. I only wished Grandpa taught me the samurai moves sooner. I start to grab my necklace in retrospection of the time it saved my life. The force field that protected me from the aircraft debris was real. I know it was real. I hope that force field will protect me again.

The bus finally arrives to Mount Tenchi and the temperature is mighty cold. I purposely keep my distance from Tam and try to avoid eye contact with him. The tour guide begins his history lesson about the significance of the mountain.

"Welcome to Mount Tenchi! This is a special mountain where the mystery and magic are alive! The myth of the two dragons and the samurai from the skies that rescues the village that was once here. Come follow me!"

The tour guide is full of energy and enthusiasm, but my classmates are awfully apathetic and aloof. With no shame, my classmates are crying "this is boring" and "I want to go home". While my classmates are whining, I tune out into paranoia. I am thinking about my life being in danger. Tam is a type of person that would kill someone and get away with it. Total disregard for anyone because he's a spoiled and privilege person that thinks everything is entitled to him. By punching him, I made him feel mortal in front his peers which hurt his fragile pride. As we trudge up the hill, I become more paranoid and anticipate the worst from Tam.

The tour guide stops the class midway of the mountain to explain the historical significance of the mountain. There is a cave that is very murky and mysterious.

"Hey, Jen High! Remember the two dragons? Well, those notorious monsters appeared here from this cave. Legend says that two dragons named "Fire" and "Lightening". These two dragons were disturbed by the noise from a village down in the valley because they were celebrating New Year's Day. Fireworks brightened the skies and euphoria of the people was contagious. Though the people were in full jubilance, the dragons were angry and miserable. In full wrath, the two dragons decided to attack the village without warning by flaming the homes with blistering, hot fire. Some perished from this ordeal, but a savior arose to the occasion. It was a metallic samurai that ascended from the sky! Yes, the sky! The samurai landed on top of Mount Tenchi and flew down to the village to save the people."

"He flew? That sounds like a load of bull..." said Tam.

"Watch your language Tam! Sorry sir, you can continue with your tour guide." said Mr. Zaki.

"Where was I? Oh, yes, he did indeed come from the skies and rescued the village. There's a conspicuous mystery to this legendary story. No one knows where the metal samurai came from. No one knows what town or what family he belongs to. The only facts that the historians discover are the ancient legends that the metal samurai ascends from the heavens and protected hundreds of people from two monsters through published books from its time. Legends say that the villagers built a statue in the mountain to honor the metal samurai. However, we did not find it yet or it could be just a legend."

"Can we enter the cave?" I said.

"No, it's off limits for visitors. It's very unsafe and there are multiple pitfalls that will lead you to your death. We will continue the tour up the mountain."

I become slightly disappointed that I couldn't go into the cave, but curiosity is creeping in my mind. As the class group moves up the mountain, I decide to ignore the tour guide's commands and snuck into the gloomy cave. My cell phone becomes my flashlight to see if I can find the mysterious statue. I yell "HELLO" and a vibrant echo awakens the dark cave. Bats start flying out and one of the flying fur balls hit my hand. My cell phone flies out and hits the ground. The cell phone shatters into a million pieces and I succumb into total darkness. I immediately regret this poor decision of going into the cave and become scared shitless. How am I going to get out of here? Shaking and quivering from the cave cold temperatures and fearing that I won't make it out alive from this cave. Suddenly, I hear a sinister laugh and I start running!

"Oh, my god! It's the metal samurai!" I scream with fear.

With no aim of direction, I am running in a pitch-black cave as fast I can to escape the metal samurai, but I get trip over by an unknown object. BAM! I land face first and in full pain. The laugh gets louder and louder but becomes oddly familiar. It is not the metal samurai; it is just Tam!

"Oh, my god the metal samurai…you are such a little bitch. Ha! Ha!" said Tam.

Tam isn't alone. He is with five other guys from Jen High who were jerks like him. They were all laughing like hyenas at me, and I am embarrassed with shame.

"Why are you in the cave?" I ask.

"Hafu, I am here for retribution." Tam said.

"Retribution?" I said with caution.

"Ah, yes. Retribution is indeed a necessity in life. You publicly humiliated me in front of the school, and I want you accept your punishment."

"You wrecked my bike and I almost was expelled from school because of you! What else do you want?"

"I want you expelled from life. I want you to disappear like you didn't exist. Do you know who I am? I am the wealthiest student at Jen High. I come from a prestigious background of great men while you come from a rice field. You're worthless and shall die upon my hands. We don't need any more charity cases in our school. You're not even full Japanese, Hafu! I am going to do the proper courtesy of wiping you off from the face of this earth. Death is the suitable punishment for you."

"You are kidding right? You know you will go to jail if you kill me, right?"

"Didn't you read my note? I meant those words. Besides, who will believe a poor farmer boy over me? My father is connected to all levels and hierarchy of law enforcement. We donate millions of yen to all police officers for their service. Killing you will be the easy part."

"Tam, what the hell? Are you really trying to commit murder? Because I punched you? Isn't that a little extreme?"

"Not murder but doing the right thing for Jen High by exterminating the useless excrement that devalues our school name. I am a god and you cursed my name! Boys, kick his ass!"

The five guys begin crushing me with fury of punches and kicks. The flurries of fist and feet left me with a both eyes swollen shut. It is difficult to breathe because one of my ribs broke. Every area of my body, I feel aching pain. Morbidly, I am beginning to think that my life is about to end.

"Wait! Stop hitting Hafu. It's my turn. Pick his pathetic ass up." said Tam.

I could barely see with my right eye and my mouth is overflowing with blood.

"You know what? I have a creative idea. Let's drag Hafu at the edge over there." said Tam with a sinister tone.

The five guys drag me to the edge of the cave and there is a steep incline. At the bottom, there are sharp and jagged rocks that can cut through a Kobe steak.

"Stand him up." said Tam.

Tam punches me in the stomach harder than usual and I cough up more blood.

"Hafu, it was nice knowing you. Torturing your soul was fun for a while but you decided to bite back. Very admirable but you do not fuck with Tam, the god! We will tell Mr. Zaki that I tried to stop you from entering the cave, but you vehemently ignored my commands and went inside anyways. I will throw down to the sharp rocks, so you can be a kebob. See you in hell!"

"Fuck you!" I said while blood lands on his white shirt.

"You ruined my favorite shirt! Time to die...... Wait, what's on your neck?"

Tam sees my father's necklace and attempts to grab the medallion.

"Since you won't need this, I'll take your precious jewelry home as a souvenir for my first kill!"

Tam wraps his devilish fingers on the medallion but suddenly, the medallion begins to activate with a teal bright light!

"What the f..." said Tam.

The medallion creates a strong force that tosses Tam and his gang back a hundred feet and instills tremendous amount of fear within Tam. The light is engulfing and bright that illuminates the entire cave.

"Fellas, I think it's time to leave!" said Tam cowardly.

Tam and the gang run with fright and leave the cave to a safe haven. On the contrary, I am hardly standing on my two feet with multiple lacerations, bruises, and bleeding like the Niagara Falls. Gingerly, I attempt to walk forward but I am too weak to move an inch. I fall backwards, and my body starts sliding into the incline! Headfirst; I am sliding directly towards the sharp stones anticipating an excruciating and agonizing death.

Abruptly, the medallion activates once more and generates a portal which blocks the jagged rocks. I enter the portal which transfers me into a different area of the cave. The light from the medallion begins to coat over my whole my body and I am miraculously healed! No lacerations, bruises, and my bleeding stopped! I am suddenly confused and perplexed what just transpired.

This area of cave isn't normal nor looks like anything ordinary. The walls are covered with extraterrestrial hieroglyphics which glows in gold and silver. Water is surrounding the area that appears to be mystic and enchanting. The floor is made out of silver-steel in checkered patterns with a large strange symbol that resembles the medallion. I start to feel the chains of my necklace moving and it begins to levitate off my head. The medallion hovers towards the symbol and the cave starts to rumble! I become incredibly nervous and anxious anticipating the worst. As the medallion floats in midair, the floor tiles open and a statue rises from ground!

"Is that the legendary statue of the metal samurai?" I said.

Indeed, it is the metal samurai! The legends are true, and I am stunned with amazement. The statue resembles a samurai warrior, but it is not like a typical samurai. It is over six feet tall and commands a valiant presence. The faceplate and helmet were very robotic and futuristic. On the back of the statue were wings that reminds me of an F-16 jet with detailed designs and bizarre symbols. Samurais usually wear *sabaton* for their feet, but the footwear is space-age like. Considering samurais existed during the 4th century, this is highly unusual! The medallion begins to flutter towards the chest area of the statue where there is a hole that is the identical shape as the necklace. The mysterious jewelry screws itself onto the statue and the statue begins to glow! The tranquil water becomes violent and splashes everywhere. The symbols on the wall shines light like a laser towards the statue. The floor changes from silver into platinum. Suddenly, the statue moves and calls my name!

"Kenji...Kenji"

"Oh my god! I am about to be killed by the metal samurai! I need to get out of here!" I said.

"Son, it's me. Your father."

"What?"

CHAPTER 4

THE GOD AWAKENS

In a flash, I am in bewilderment and consume with puzzlement. I slowly turnaround and gaze at the statue.

"My father?" I said.

"Yes, Kenji. This is your father."

The statue takes off the faceplate and it is my father's face! I begin to cry and run over to give him an emphatic hug. Tear are flowing heavier than the Nile River as it cascades towards the floor. As our embrace expires, I begin to ask a series of questions because I had plenty of answers that I need to know.

"Dad, it's been so long! I thought you died!" I said. "I have so many questions to ask you. Why are you here? Why aren't you home with Mom and me? It's been seven long and hellish years living in Japan! What the hell is going on?"

"Watch your language, Kenji."

"Sorry for my foul mouth but you have some serious explaining to do. What's up the necklace you gave me that day? Are you the legendary samurai? But what wait, aren't you an American and a pilot? How are you alive? Did you survive the plane crash and lived in this cave the whole time? What are these symbols on the walls? This doesn't make any sense. I am confused and lost and..."

"Kenji! I will provide you clarity and the substantial answers that you are requesting but I must inform you that I am not alive. I am a spirit."

"A spirit?"

"Yes, I am also a God."

"A god? Wait, you are a God? I thought Gods don't die. What kind of God, a Japanese samurai God? But you're Black American? I am Black right? Wait, does this mean I am a God? My mind is blown!"

"Son! Let me explain, I will take you to the galactic realm. Close your eyes." My father said.

"Galactic realm?"

"Shhh…"

My father puts his hand on my forehand and transmits us from the cave to outer space! Somehow, I can breathe.

"How did we get here? How are we breathing in space, Dad?"

"We are in the confines of the galactic realm that allows us to travel at any time, place or period. We can breathe in space because we are Gods."

"I am a God?"

"Yes, I will provide you all the details. Please be patient. Remember our fishing trips?"

Father and I were floating on the edge of an outlandish planet that has two rings merging with each other and multiple moons.

"This is my home planet, Alloy," said Father.

"Alloy?" I said.

"Yes, Alloy. I am neither Japanese nor African American. Matter of fact, I am not from Earth. I am an Allonian, the King of Alloy, Chief Engineer of Planets, and the creator of life. I will reveal you my true identity."

Father waves his right hand over his face and his complexation and face changes! His skin becomes metallic and his eyes are platinum!

"Whoa! Whoa! Whoa! You're all glitter!"

"Son, I know it's a lot to take in, but this is my true identity. My name is not Conway Jackson but Candor. Alloy is my beautiful planet that no human can manage to discover. We are beyond light years away from the Earth. I designed the planets that way on purpose. Alloy is a planet of steel. Unlike the steel on Earth, the steel on Alloy is organic which is used exclusively for main purposes such as land, energy, and one of the key ingredients to manufacture planets. I am the creator of all planets that you witness in the galaxy including Earth."

"Really?" I said as my jaw is dropping.

"Yes son, however, with unlimited power comes with unlimited adversity. Though the Allonians have the best quality material in all outer space, there are rivals amongst us. There are two other God tribes which are Gallos and Radilites. Millions of years ago, there were only three kingdoms. Alloy (Steel), Gallium (Iron), and Radium (Aluminum). Each kingdom lived on their individual planets that were created by the organic metals. Who made the organic metal? That is still an unsolved mystery amongst the Gods but what we do know is that these three metals form planets and our lives derived from it. Iron created the planet Gallium in which generated the Gallos tribe. Aluminum created the planet Radium in which manifested the Radilites. Steel created the planet Alloy where I and your ancestors derived from. The three kingdoms were friendly towards one another and exchanged resources to improve their planets. Imperialism was non-existent, and peace was continuously present.

I am an extension of the royal family of Alloy. King Saloh was my proud father who was tough but fair. He ruled the planet of Alloy with discipline and compassion for his people. My mother Queen Affinity was beautiful and majestic lady that I never received the chance to encounter. During her labor, my mother died after giving birth to twins. I was one of the twins."

"Wait, you are a twin which means you have brother?" I ask.

"Yes, I have a brother named Nefaric." said Candor. "My mother survived the birth when I was born but Nefaric was slightly heavier than I am which caused my mother's death. Queen Affinity could not handle the second child during labor and her body failed. I never blamed or placed a burden on Nefaric for my mother's demise but King Saloh held a lifelong grudge towards him. My father was consumed with rage and despair when mother died. He named my brother Nefaric because of her death.

Nefaric and I were born in the same palace but raised differently. My father would always favor me over Nefaric. He would groom me on how to be the next King and introduce mathematics, science, and engineering to me. Nefaric was very envious that I had a closer relationship with my father which manifested his violent tendencies. As children, Nefaric would provoke me to fight him. We would fight daily due to his insecurities and father would punish Nefaric for his transgressions. Nefaric resented me but I never resented him. I loved him and always had sympathy for his deprived needs of a father's affection.

Nefaric's life goal was to receive his father's approval. My brother would hunt Sorgas (which are equivalent to wildebeest on earth) to impress my father, but King Saloh wasn't captivated by his hunting accomplishments. Nefaric would illustrate beautiful paintings to appease my father but King Saloh ignored him. No matter how hard Nefaric tried, my father seems to not care about him. Nefaric was a reminder of his wife's death and he didn't want any part of his life. I felt bad for him and advocate to my father that Nefaric needs his tutelage. King Saloh simply refused to participate in Nefaric's life. The hostility and resentment blackened Nefaric's soul to the point he began to hate King Saloh. To release his anger and frustrations, he joined the military and became the Chief of Forces.

I was the opposite from my brother. I was infatuated when it came to study. I loved learning about our history, nature, and how planets are formed. The beauty of science was very fascinating to me. As a lad, I spend countless hours in my laboratory and create thousands of mini planets with compound chemicals found only on Alloy. After completing a galaxy, I would launch the prototype into space. My first galaxy was the Milky Way and it was simply gorgeous. My favorite planet that I generated was Earth because it was my first successful planet that I invented. It's the most dynamic planet that wasn't overheated by the star that built for the orbit. Mercury and Venus were failed experiments, but Earth survived the sun rays. I admired the multiple facets of Earth from the oceans, mountains, forest, and deserts. Unexpected life forms appeared on the planet in the result of my experiment. I watched how Earth converted from the dinosaurs to the Ice Age. When humans appeared on Earth, I was astonished about their intelligence and how they built variety of civilizations. A plethora of religions and faiths were conceived to comprehend their purpose in life and to answer their most compelling questions "why am I here?" Humans are innocent like deer and do not know their true origins which is why I never interfered. Though there are lives in different galaxies and planets with similar traits, Earth was my treasure.

As I became a young man, my main mission was to enhance Alloy as the most robust planet in the galaxy. After studying the organic steel that created the Allonians, I found unique ions that can produce solar winds which can generate energy for Alloy. The energy will be utilized for electricity, food, and weaponry for defense. I proposed a blueprint to my father, and he was highly mesmerized."

*In Alloy's Royal Quarters

"Candor, you found a great discovery. How will you harness the energy for the planet? "said King Saloh.

"I will create spheres that will hover above the stratosphere. As the spheres spin, it will collect energy from solar winds which it creates. What I will do is extract the Steel ions and place them into the sphere so maximum collections of energy can flourish. We will be the most advanced planet in the galaxy. "Candor said.

"Son, you will be an outstanding King one day. I am proud of you. I will name you "Chief of Engineering". I will assign an engineer council for your project."

"I will name the sphere, Affinity"

"Your mother would be proud."

The Affinity generated so much energy that Alloy ceased trades with Radium and Gallium. Our agriculture was thriving from the energy which produced abundance of crops. Weapons for the military improved tremendously with new aircrafts that are more cutting-edge. Scientists started new projects from this energy. I named this newfound energy "AFOP" which stands for "Advancement For Our People".

Unfortunately, the cease of trades generated hostility and envy amongst the two kingdoms in which war became foreseeable. The two Kings notice that Alloy was not sharing the new power that I discovered and craved our newfangled resource. I didn't mind creating a sphere to enhance their planet, but my father refused to share this new invention.

"We want the solar winds to generate energy for our planet!" said King of Radium.

"No, the Allonians created an invention that suits our people and I will not share it." said King Saloh.

"We had peace for many years but now you don't want to share prosperity with your neighbor planets. This type of power can be advantageous to our planets and we can become more resilient." said King of Gallium.

"I refuse to share this solar wind power with your kingdoms. I do not trust *your intentions of what you will do with this energy. It was created for our people and our people only. This is not up for negotiation." said King Saloh.*

"Then so be it. You will feel my retribution. I will declare war!" said King of Radium.

"I declare war too. Once we obliterate the Allonian people, I will come for your planet, King Radium." said King of Gallium.

"War is what you desire? Fine, we will fight to the death!" said King Saloh.

"My father for the first time went to Nefaric for help. He wanted him to mobilize the troops."

"Nefaric, you need to mobilize the troops now! War is upon us and we need your services." said King Saloh.

"Father, it will be an honor to lead the Allonians to glory. I will assemble the soldiers and prepare for this epic battle. I hope to make you proud." said Nefaric.

"Just do it now! We don't have the duration for the soliloquys. Planet Radium and Gallium are on their way to attack our precious Alloy. Go, go I say!" said King Saloh.

"Yes father, I will do as you command." said Nefaric.

"Nefaric mobilized the troops as Gallos and Radilites bomb our cities and palace. Lasers and explosions were ubiquitous. Gallos used an aerial fleet while the Radilites used ground troops. The Allonians had both superior aerial and ground troops to counter the enemies' attacks. Destruction was becoming the new norm and agonies of my people were damaging. City skyscrapers were falling and crumbling. Smoke was drifting throughout the planet which smothered the skies. Thousands of the Allonians perished from the ambush. Fortunately, the Allonians defeated the Gallos and Radilites in the first battle but my brother wanted more blood to be shed. Nefaric discussed his brutal sentiments with my father and me in our palace chambers.

"Father, we won the battle but let's annihilate their planets now! "said Nefaric.

"I will concur. We shall attack their planets first thing in the morning!" said King Saloh.

King Saloh and Nefaric kept deliberating their plans of annihilation and genocide. I became alarmed from the idea of wiping out the generations of Gods. AFOP was an idea for Alloy originally but I discovered something major in my laboratory while war was being conducted. I mentioned with an alternative plan and mentioned the idea to my father.

"No, father! I found a new discovery! There are ions in iron and aluminum. With the combination of all three, we can generate one hundred times more energy than with steel alone. Let's stop the violence. We are stronger when we are united as Gods. I feel responsible for this ordeal. I thought I was helping my planet, but I helped destroy it. This new discovery can end all this war and we can formulate a peace treaty; hence we can trade again but most importantly gain new energy for all three planets." said Candor.

"Candor, you are speaking like a diplomat. Your forward thinking will create more harmony than hate. This war should not have happened, and I will take full accountability. I will contact the Kings and start a peace treaty." said King Saloh.

"Father! They came to our planet and killed our people! You are just going to let them have a pass?" said Nefaric.

"I gave you a pass when you came to this world and slain my wife! I can give compassion when necessary which is this very moment. It was a fallacy to enter the war in the first place. Gods should not go against each other. I will cease this war. Nefaric, your mission is complete. You are relieved from duty." said King Saloh.

"I am tired of being the burden of your pain. It is not fair that mother died because I was born. I gave you my honor in battle and put my life on the line for the legacy of my family and Alloy, but this is how you repay me? Father, why do you hate me? I do not deserve this torment!" said Nefaric.

"I said you're relieved from duty. As the King of Alloy and your father, the services that your provide are no longer needed. Please leave at once." said King Saloh.

"Candor, you stole my honor, glory, and thunder. One day I will be King!" said Nefaric.

"No, you won't be King. I have already decided who is worthy to lead Alloy to the brighter future and take this lovely planet into the horizons of fortune. It is Candor who has the integrity, intelligence, and foresight that you will never possess. You will support Candor when my time has passed and be his assistant." said King Saloh.

"Father, I am finished attempting to gain your approval from you. I have a realization that I will never live up to your daunting and unrealistic

expectations and always be in the shadows of Candor. Your precious Candor caused this whole war, yet he gets amnesty for his transgressions. I will not tolerate this berating, ridicule, and double standard from you ever again. Mark my words." said Nefaric.

"Nefaric stormed out of the King's quarters with haste and never returned. I ventured back to my laboratory to dissect the ions from the three metals. With the combination of ions, solar winds can generate massive amount of energy. I realize that the ions must be separated at 33% before fusing. If all three ions are over 33%, then the ions will cause a chain reaction like a nuclear weapon. Diligently, I wrote my lab notes into my journal and met with my father at his chambers."

"Father, why are you so hard on Nefaric? He saved Alloy and he was following your command."

"Nefaric reminds me of the death of your mother. I can't bear to look at him. He's a menace and always will be. I don't trust him, and neither shall you."

"Father, I think you should display some compassion. At least say "thank you" for his service because he indeed put his life on the line for you and others. He's a hero, not a villain. I think you should apologize."

"Candor, I have been harsh towards him and I will try to discuss peace with him on another day. Let's talk about this treaty."

I told my father about each Radium and Gallium should only produce 33% of the metals to create the Affinity Spheres during trades. The AFOP ACT is a treaty for separations of power. This treaty indicates that the AFOP should only be used for the people and exclude military operations with this energy. There will be three engineers from each planet that will be the gatekeepers of the ions and will distribute the energy when all three engineers are together. I will be one of the gatekeepers and the Kings from Radium and Gallium must select a worthy engineer to help harness this energy.

"This treaty is beautifully written. I will invite all three Kings to my courts." said King Saloh.

"The three Kings met, and all agreed with the treaty. Signatures were signed, and the wars deceased. King Saloh called all of Allonians to his palace as he conducted his speech from his balcony."

"Today, we stand in unity. We will become one. Many of you lost love

ones through violence and savagery. I am sorry for their losses. It pains me to hear and know that death was present on our lands. With the AFOP Act, we will unite with Radium and Gallium to regain peace and tranquility. Love always conquers hate."

*crowd cheers

I met the two engineers from Radium and Gallium in my laboratory and taught them how to build the Affinity. Radium's engineer was Zerk and Gallium engineer was Ollo. The ions were stored into the medallions for protection from cross contamination. I programmed the medallions with a force field for defense, healing capabilities, and warrior suit that is equipped with sword and glove blasters. Part of treaty was a non-disclosure agreement between the Kings and engineers about the medallion attributes being known to the public. If the public knew these capabilities, it could start controversy and chaos."

"That makes sense now!" I said. "The medallion saved my life and healed me. Glove blasters? Sounds like a weapon. Wait, I thought the treaty said you can't use the AFOP for military operations."

"Operations for weaponry but for self-defense, it was legal. I programmed the medallion to activate with only with Ollo, Zerk and Alloy royal DNA hence why the medallion saved your life, Kenji." said Candor.

"Though most Gods believed in the AFOP Act, there were always Gods that did not agree with the policy including my brother. Nefaric lurked and eavesdropped into my laboratory and heard the special attributes that the medallion obtained. He became very curious and had a plethora of questions.

"I read the transcript of the AFOP Act and it says that only 33% of the ions shall be used before fusion. Why?" said Nefaric.

"Nefaric, it will cause a catastrophic explosion and abolish everything we know." said Candor.

"Really? Can you use the AFOP on our military weaponry?" said Nefaric.

"Yes, however, the treaty will ban such use. The AFOP Act specially states that no ions shall ever…..."

"Brother, relax. I know I read the transcript, simply curious that's all. May I see your gloves?"

"Why and for what, Nefaric."

"I want to see how the gloves perform in action."

"No, I don't want anyone to use it."

* Nefaric snatches gloves

"Hey! Give it back now!"

"Don't worry. I am going to utilize these gloves out in the open field"

"Nefaric utilizes the glove blasters towards the window and shot a beam towards one of the Affinity. The sphere exploded, and debris sparkled down to the ground like shooting stars."

"Nefaric! You could have caused a major catastrophe to our planet! What the hell were you thinking?"

"I am thinking this is a useful instrument for my military. This is only 33% of Steel ions? Imagine using the fusion with iron and aluminum ions with these gloves. I can be the ultimate God! You wanted to keep this power all to yourself, didn't you?"

"Zerk and Ollo became edgy and unnerved. I started to lash out on Nefaric.

"I made the treaty rules to keep others away from the AFOP. I do not want the AFOP energy used for tyranny and destruction. AFOP is for the people, not for individual power."

"I think it is very asinine to suppress this form of power and not use its full potential. I will get all three ions and I will rule Alloy as the rightful King!"

"Father appointed me to be the next successor. I am sorry brother; it's not in your future."

"You are nothing but a brown-nosing scumbag! I don't see how he favors you over me! You will give me the ions and I will give you until tomorrow to change your mind before I will change it for you!"

"Is that a threat?"

"Threats are pending actions waiting to happen. This is coercive gesture on the bounds of the foreseeable. See you tomorrow and I will see those gloves fully equip with the AFOP at the maximum level. Please do not take my request lightly."

*throws gloves in Candor's face and leaves the laboratory

"I need to repair the force field."

"I immediately told my father about the Nefaric's threats, but he didn't take my concerns seriously."

"Candor, he is just a big infant that cries all the time. You don't have to worry, son."

"*Father, I am worried about Nefaric. You might be right about trusting him. I don't trust him now and he's becoming very power hungry.*"

"*Candor, I have been King for a long time and there's nothing that alarms me, especially Nefaric. Get some sleep, we have to deliver the people a speech about your Affinity progress.*"

"*Yes, father.*"

"For precaution, I took all the ions and placed into three medallions. I requested Zerk and Ollo to enter my chambers for risk management."

"*Listen Zerk and Ollo, I think my brother will attempt to steal our ions for something malevolent. I finished the medallions. Please protect your ions with your life because I am getting a premonition that something wrong will transpire.*"

"*Candor, why not send him to prison chambers tonight? He destroyed the Affinity which against the law!* "*said Zerk.*

"*Nefaric threatened you. I think that is enough evidence to pursue court martial.*" *said Ollo.*

"*I cannot honor that request. It's above my pay grade.*"

"*What? Tell your father now! He is trying to sabotage our plan and our planets signed that treaty.* "*said Zerk.*

"*I think Zerk is correct. He seems to be unstable.* "*said Ollo.*

"*I can't Zerk and Ollo. He is not only my brother and my father's son, but he is a war hero for the planet Alloy. This will not please the masses if I persecute my own brother. I implemented full capacity of ions in each medallion. Please return to your home planets so the AFOP is safe.*"

"*But you just said that he may do something malevolent.* "*said Ollo.*

"*I think we should take action now!*" *said Zerk.*

"*This is my action, just take the medallions and return to your home planets. Please honor my request.*"

"*Yes, Candor.*" *said Zerk.*

"*As you wish.*" *said Ollo*

"The next morning, father, two Kings and I were broadcasting the updated version of Affinity's to Alloy people. On the palace balcony, father and the two kings were preparing to deliver the gigantic news to the people.

"*Hello my Allonians! I am standing next to King Radium and King Gallium. As we stand side by side as equals, there was a resolution of peace and progression. I present you the Affinity, named after my lovely wife. With the combinations of chemical compounds, this sphere will provide energy for all three planets. Launch the sphere!"*

Candor: "The Affinity was launched into the skies and the Allonians were amazed by its wonders. I was excited but anxious as I watched my prototype finally into its operation phase. As the Affinity was reaching the stratosphere, the sphere exploded from a missile attack by Nefaric! The crowd became frightened and worried. Nefaric was standing on top of a tall building that was adjacent to palace and echoed his sentiments."

"Alloy, this Prince Nefaric. I will shed some truth and wisdom upon you! This Affinity shall never happen because it's from the blood of your love ones. The three Kings signed a non-disclosure agreement and withholding information from the people!"

*crowd gets confused and murmuring

"Yes, we signed a non-disclosure agreement but it's for the greater good. Why did you destroy the Affinity? It's for the people! "yelled King Saloh.

"Was it the greater good with King Radium and Gallium killed our people? Is the AFOP worth the lives of fathers, mothers, sons, and daughters? They are planning to eradicate Allonians with the energy. With the three ions at full maximum capacity, the three Kings will commit genocide if anyone will question their authority! You are keeping information from us, you are not fit to be king, father!"

*crowd gets angry

"Speak the truth! Speak the truth!"

"Do not listen to Nefaric, he was not involved with this project. These are all lies and Nefaric is committing treason. The non-disclosure information shall remain amongst the Kings."

"Tell that my son that died! "yelled a fellow Allonian.

"I lost my husband because of those Kings!" cried Allonian woman.

*crowd gets very hostile

"I say Alloy deserves a new King." Said Nefaric. "We do not need liars and incompetence. We do not need leaders keeping the truth from their people. My father placed Candor as the next King to take over the planet because he's a pathological liar as well! He is holding all the ions for himself and possesses weaponry which is a violation of the treaty! That is true treason!"

*crowd is restless

"Stop the fabrications!" yelled King Saloh. "We do not want anyone to have full power of the ions because it can lead to a nuclear reaction. That is the truth! Nefaric, you are an embarrassment to this planet, and you committed the ultimate betrayal. Guards, seize him at once!"

"Send the guards, I don't care but the Allonians still remember the deaths of their significant others because you didn't want to share the AFOP. Your decision-making cost us lives! I say we get the ions from Candor and make a nuclear-powered bomb to destroy Gallium and Radium! We need a revolution, now!"

crowd cheers "Get the ions! Get the ions!

"The people were galvanized by Nefaric's fabrications and populism. Masses of people started attack the palace."

"Father, let's get out here!"

"Yes, we need to find a haven. Let's go gentlemen!"

As we turnaround, we were blocked by the thousands of guards!

"Wait, why are you blocking our advancement! The Allonians are revolting and we need to escape! I order you to move as once. "said King Saloh.

"You are no longer my King. I take orders from King Nefaric." said the Head Guard.

"What? I am the King of Alloy."

"You committed treason and I am ordered to execute all four of you from King Nefaric. Guards take out your swords." said the Head Guard.

"What the hell is this?" questioned King Saloh with great concern.

"By the orders of King Nefaric, I sentence King Radium, King Gallium, King Saloh, and Prince Candor to death due to treason, murder, and mendacious actions."

Candor: "Before the guards began their execution, I activated the medallion to retrieve the warrior suit. The force field was still not working and the guards advanced forward. King Radium and Gallium died instantly from the impaling swords. The Guards were about to execute my father, but I utilized the glove blaster and shot a powerful beam. An enormous explosion erupted but the shield finally functioned and protected my father and me. The warrior suit has flying capabilities, so I carried my father to safety. We soared into the mountains where no one can find him.

"Stay here father, I have to travel to Gallium and Radium now before Nefaric gets to Zerk and Ollo. I must warn them." Candor said.

"Ok, son. Be safe. Do not return." King Saloh said.

"Why not, Father? I am worried that Nefaric will find you and take your life."

"The ions are too important for our people including our neighbor planets. We shall not allow or permit Nefaric to get his evil hands on the ions. He will use the ions for power and oppression towards all three planets. Take the ions somewhere beyond our realm."

"But Father..."

"It's an order from your King and father. Please complete this noble deed for the future of Alloy."

"Yes, my lord."

Candor: "I kiss my father's ring and we embraced for the last time. It was the final time that I saw my father. I don't know if he's alive or deceased, but I remained optimistic that he's still breathing.

In full panic, I hovered into the stratosphere to planet Radium and Gallium to warn Zerk and Ollo about my planet's quagmire. With vital information and details, I thoroughly explained the assassinations, and both were flabbergasted and in disbelief. I told Zerk and Ollo to escape their home planets with the medallions and come with me to Earth, a planet that's undetected and off the grid. Both agreed, and we escaped to Earth. I have a spacecraft hangar on a hidden moon which is located between Alloy and Radium. All three of us escaped into my spacecraft, the 'COMET FLARE' and transported to Earth.

The space journey to Earth was tumultuous, dangerous, and frightening. We navigated and avoided meteor showers during the voyage which caused minor damage towards the COMET FLARE. The asteroid belt was the most challenging to travel through and as utilized weaponry to surpass the obstacle. COMET FLARE has strong weaponry with energy beams which blasted through the belt. After passing Mars, I see the beautiful creation that I assembled years ago. I gazed in bewilderment and engulfed by a surreal feeling while landing on the planet that I made. We land safely in Japan on a mountain which is known as Mount Tenchi today. The year was 378 A.D., the Kofun Period. It was nighttime and we formed a camp inside the mountain. The COMET FLARE was stored into my medallion and we began to create habitation inside Mount Tenchi.

Due to our superior technology, our habitat was formed in ten seconds and we rested until morning.

The next day, I stood on top of the mountain. The sun was lively and bright which verified the nickname "the rising sun". As I gazed down the mountain, I witnessed a celebration down the valley. It was some formation of a parade of Japanese people. At first, I was admiring the natural life that was functioning in autonomous matter. There were loud drum rhythms and music being orchestrated in the air. I heard children laughing, women dancing, and elders enjoying the festivities. The people reminded me of Alloy, and I could sense their happiness and bliss. My creation formed into a living and breathing planet unlike any other planet that I assembled. I didn't imagine this to happen and thought it would a vacant planet with no life forms existing, but the organic steel manifested a diversity of life which produced humans. It's simply beautiful and I was enthralled to examine more about Earth.

As I continued to observe the parade, I noticed something strange. Two odd looking creatures which resembled dragons was participating in the festival, but it wasn't an animal but people in costume. Suddenly, the people inside the dragons removed their costumes and attacked the innocent people! They were not part of the festival but raiders on a mission to destruction. I began to have flashbacks when Alloy was attacked by our adversaries. I witnessed homicides of innocent people from elders to infants which boiled my blood into an oblivion. There were about fifty raiders who possessed sharp kitanas and torches. The raiders were burning the homes and causing total chaos with no remorse. Hearing the screams of anguish and pain disturbed me. I may not know the circumstances or complexities on why the raiders decided to attack this particular village, but there's no justification to murder. I activated my medallion, assembled the warrior suit, and glided down the mountain to end the terror.

In startling fashion, I landed into the village like an eagle swooping for its prey. All fifty raiders suspended their terroristic acts and stood still with authentic fear. I drew my sword which made up Allonian-steel and the blade was pure sapphire-plasma. The pupils of my mask glowed emerald-green which elevates my vision. I increased my ion power to thirty-seven percent and prepared to eliminate every raider in the vicinity. One raider charged at me with his kitana and roared 'shinu made no jikan' (time to die). I waited patiently as he was aiming his murderous sword towards my heart, but I did not hold a particle of distress. Humans can't kill a God. The kitana strikes my chest plate, bends into a u-shape, and impaled the raider's neck. The raider perished hastily and fell to the ground. The other raiders trembled in fear and attempted to run away like the yellow-bellied cowards that they were, but I didn't accept their destination to safety. The "gravitational heave" are one of the features that the warrior suit possessed. The original purpose of the gravitational heave was for transportation of heavy metal masses by manipulating the gravity. In this case, I am using it for pure annihilation. I utilized this power and lifted all forty-nine members into the stratosphere. I navigated into the skies and organized the raiders in a single file line. One by one, I used my sword to be them into a permanent slumber with one swing at a time. Then, I used the gravitational heave one last time to ship their lifeless bodies into space and finishing the deed with a glove-blasting beam."

"That was bad ass," I said.

"I should say 'watch your language' but you are right, it was. Shall I continue my story?" said Candor.

"Yes, go on Father." I said.

Candor: "This was the first that I utilized violence for solving a problem. I am usually a pacifist, but sometimes evil must be dealt with by force. This was always the mindset of my brother. He always thought violence was the answer. I think violence was only essential when there's no more choices but to fight back. However, in that moment, I felt like my brother Nefaric as I used savagery methods to end a threat. I wasn't remorseful though because I felt like it was necessary after witnessing the atrocities down the valley. I hover down to the village and was introduced by an applause from the people. Some were afraid of me, but some embraced my presence. A small child ran up to me and hugged my leg. That's when I realized that I did something greater than myself. It wasn't being a God or creating planets that fulfilled me. It was protecting the defenseless against evil doers that gave me purpose. As I turn around, I see Zerk and Ollo approaching me."

*Top of Mount Tenchi

"Are you okay, Candor" said Zerk.

"I heard a lot of commotion, what is going?" said Ollo.

"I am fine. I think we should be guardians to these humans. They are young species that need tutelage, but I want to remain anonymous to study their habits, cultures, and ecosystems."

"I like that idea sir, but I want to go back to home planet." said Zerk.

"So, do I, Candor. I don't want to be on this planet. There's no purpose here. My family are back at Gallium," said Ollo

"We can't go back! We can't give Nefaric the power of the ions!" I said.

"I will give you my ion. I have a wife and three daughters. I shall not leave them be," said Zerk.

"I rather die in honor than live as a coward," said Ollo.

"It's not being a coward; it's finding a solution before we can counterattack Nefaric. Earth possess some resources that can destroy Nefaric. I know it! I created this planet and there's natural agriculture in which none of our home planet obtains. We just need time to discover it and use it for our advantage."

"Sorry, Candor. I have to return to Radium. "said Zerk.

"I have to return as well. "said Ollo.

"Hand me the ions and take the COMET FLARE now. If you need to go, then leave. You will regret this decision."

"The only regret I have been agreeing to the AFOP Act, "said Zerk.

"I concur. Let's go home Zerk," said Ollo.

Candor: "Zerk and Ollo could not fathom my vision. They didn't comprehend that they are signing their own death sentences. Zerk and Ollo transferred the ions into my medallion and left Earth. It was the final time that I saw Zerk and Ollo. As they left the atmosphere, I continued to help the people at the village. There were lifeless bodies from the raiders' murders permeates all over the village. There's a key molecule in all humans that derives from the Allonians that I can restore only one time and it was feasible to bring them back to life. About 150 people perished but with my healing abilities, all 150 were able to breathe again. The people were thankful and honored me with a large feast. My first time ever eating sushi and rice. The people treated me like family and I appreciative of their hospitality. As a gift to the people, I created a river for the humans to use for fresh water. I disappeared into the mountains and began my studies inside Mount Tenchi.

I remained on Earth. Although I had enough ions to defeat my brother, it wasn't enough to restore all three planets. Alloy was damaged beyond repair and I can't renovate the planet completely without discovering a new component to rectify it. I chose to stay on Earth, so I can defeat evil but also restore the life on Alloy. I do not conduct actions in haste, I am patient. Calculations matter."

"So, the story was true! The two dragons weren't dragons but raiders using Trojan tactics to invade a village and you saved them. Holy cow! What year was it? That had to be over 1000 years ago!, "I said.

Candor: "Just about. One day in Alloy is 500 years on Earth, I was privileged to witness many historical moments in human history. The evolution of people was astonishing to me. I lived in Mount Tenchi most of my time here, but I did indeed travel to other regions to study human behaviors, customs, and moralities. One of the abilities of being a God is to be able to adapt to the environment. Incognito was my technique to examine humans without interference. Like a chameleon, I transformed into different complexions depending on the region, era, and time. I lived through the medieval times with King Henry, Roman Empire, Ottoman Empire, Mongol Conquest, Napoleon Wars, War of the Roses, British Empire, American Revolution War, Mexican War of Independence, American Civil War, The Boxer Rebellion, The Great War, World War II, Korean War, Cold War, Vietnam War, and many more. I didn't interfere with the outcomes in war because humans must learn from their history and atrocities.

Also, I learned that the human spirit is immensely powerful. Despite the discrimination or segregation in which some societies place on their differences, those who are oppressed fought for their right to be equal. The Americans fought the British due unfair taxation and creating a new nation based upon freedoms of man. I witnessed the Civil Rights Movement with Martin Luther King Jr. which warmed my heart and soul. A man without any supernatural powers making a profound impact for equality for his people.

After examining the human world for quite some time, I became somewhat lonely. As a god, I can live for a long duration, but humans don't live as long. I made many friendships along the journey but all of them perish while I remain standing. The human life cycle constantly changes, and it was something I wasn't accustomed as an Allonian. It was an intriguing experience but a melancholy one. As times changed, so did people.

I still haven't found the resource to restore Alloy and defeat my brother. It became frustrating and hopeless. One of my experiments was separating the ions and implementing each ion in separate continents to generate power. Iron (from Gallium) was placed in North America and Metallic (from Radium) was placed in Africa while Steel (from Alloy) was in Japan. Usually, separation of ions generates massive power through kinetic charges, but it failed. If I returned to Alloy, I would be a dead God. If I stayed, I felt that I was neglecting my duties as the next King of Alloy.

I just didn't know what to do. To feel some form of honor, I decided to join the United States Air Force to become a pilot. It gave me some sense of integrity and accountability. As a disguise, I transformed into a human and went by the name Conway Jackson. Pilot training was rudimentary and navigating an F-16 was primitive. Human technology was very mediocre compared to what I am accustomed to, but it was necessary to blend in the culture. I requested to be stationed in Japan to be near Mount Tenchi and my request was granted.

After serving the Air Force for a few months, I decided to explore outside the base to eat some noodles at local shop downtown Kobe and that's where I met your mother. She was beautiful and humble. After spending centuries on Earth, there wasn't a woman as precious and special as her. Every man desires a woman whether you are a God or not. My priorities changed when I met Timokko. I wanted a family and peaceful life. When you were born, I knew you would have a genius intellect."

"Whoa, let me stop you there." I said. "I don't know if you were paying attention while you died, but I really suck at school. I had to leave the military base and learn at a Japanese school. I can barely speak the language and just getting by with grades. I feel idiotic and incompetent."

"Kenji, you are an Allonian." Candor said." We have superior intellect compared to the humans. I planted a device in your brain to harness your intelligence. I wanted you to grow up as a normal human and fit in society. I gave you an IQ 110. Allonians IQ are 1000 or above."

"Wait a second, you basically dumbed me down?" I said with vex.

"In a sense, somewhat but I didn't want you to standout or end up like an outsider." Candor said. "I just wanted you to be a normal child. You have strong intelligence as a human, but I will enhance your learning capabilities. Allonians can learn anything from a simple touch of your hand. Grab a book and you can process and download the information within five seconds. I will remove this handicap device from your brain."

My father placed his hand my head and I heard a click inside my head.

"Speak Japanese."

"Huh?"

"Speak Japanese now."

"Watashi wa sore o okonau koto ga dekimasen…. hey! I can speak it fluently! Holy cow!"

"You have the ability to speak all the languages in the world including Allonian. I transferred all the knowledge that I learned over the years to you. With the removal of the device, you will also have superior strength. Try lifting that boulder from the ground."

"I am weak there's no way I can do this."

"Son, just do the task."

I walk over to the boulder that is eight feet high. I put my two hands on it and thrust up the boulder like a pebble.

"Holy smokes! I am Hercules!"

"Not quite but you're real. Allonians have extraordinary strength. I only implemented the device, so you wouldn't overpower your peers both intellectually and physical strength. Also, you have superior reaction and instincts. You can dodge a silver bullet at point blank range. I was going to remove the device once you became a man, but I was assassinated."

"Assassinated? How? I saw a ray of energy hitting your F-16 and there wasn't anyone around?"

"Yes, because the energy beam that hit my F-16 was Allonian power, not human. The Nefaric is the only Allonian to utilize that type of weapon which is called "Chemo-Lightning". It's deadly accurate and so fast that humans would never be able to see it with a trained eye. I don't know how he discovered Earth, but that attack was from a distance. Maybe, Zerk and Ollo revealed my location. That's my only assumption."

"This makes more sense why I was the only person who saw the

Chemo-Lightning. Which means he's coming here for the medallion! Would he use that attack again?"

"Yes, son. I need you to protect that medallion. I have a feeling he just wanted to eliminate me, but I highly doubt he would use that attack again. It could destroy a planet if there's a direct hit on the Earth's crust. You must defeat Nefaric once he approaches to Earth. You have all my research and studies implemented in your brain. I haven't found the resource to give the ions power to restore Alloy, but you must conquer that labyrinth. Earth does have the resource, but I couldn't discover it. This is your time, son."

"I will fulfill that promise. I wonder why Nefaric didn't come to Earth sooner to retrieve the medallion."

"I don't know. Perhaps, he was terrified of my warrior suit and wanted to kill me from a distance. It's a peculiar and spineless strategy. Remember, 500 years is only a day for the Allonians. Nefaric will be coming soon and he is relentless…."

Kenji, my son, I apologize that I retained this secret about Alloy from you. I wanted to tell you when you became a young man. Also, I didn't expect to perish in an unexpected matter. I will be here in Mount Tenchi because my spirit only allows me to be designated in one area. Allonian by-laws are: "where you perish is where you remain". Though I perished on the flight line, I created a spirit channel to Mount Tenchi prior to my death.

I will guide you and impart the Allonian customs. This will be your retreat haven if you need more resources for the Warrior suit. Take the medallion everywhere you travel. You will never know when danger may appear. You must go, your teacher will be worried about you. Take care and god speed."

"Is there anyway a God can come back to life? We need you back on Earth, especially Mom."

"That's something that I don't believe is possible. With the transferred knowledge, you can discover the cure to bring Gods back to life. I do miss your mother dearly and I know she is still in sorrow. However, you must not tell her about our encounter. It's simply better that way. As of now, I will be here at Mount Tenchi, go now.

"Yes, sir."

We embraced one more time and my father turned back into a statue. The metal samurai goes underground, and the cave walls suddenly glistens a bright light. The light surrounds my body and transports me back outside the cave.

CHAPTER 5

DOES FEAR CREATES RESPECT?

"Kenji! Where the heck did you go young man? The whole class was worried sick about your disappearance. Tam told the class that you went inside the cave!" said Mr. Zaki.

"No, I was just using the bathroom. Sorry that I didn't ask permission, but I had to go. Too much to eat." I said.

"Eww, too much info Kenji! Ok, but next time, raise your hand so we can have full accountability. Get back with the class." said Mr. Zaki.

As I return to my classmates, I noticed that Tam had a brand-new t-shirt from the gift shop. He must've thrown away the blood stain shirt with my DNA all over it. This bastard really attempted to cover up a murder. Tam didn't know that I am still alive until I tap his chunky shoulder.

"Remember me?" I said.

Tam and his goon posse were so petrified like he saw a ghost. Their vacant expressions on their faces were priceless.

"What the fu…"

"Tam, watch your language!" said Mr. Zaki. "Ok, class listen up! Aboard the bus right now, time to go home."

As I aboard the bus, I saw Amaya's seat is open again. This is my golden opportunity to sit with this beautiful girl. Amaya waves at me and ask to sit with her. As I am walking down the aisle, Tam is blocking my path to Amaya.

"Hafu, I don't know how you are still alive, but we will finish you after the ride."

"Get out of my way, Tam." I said.

"Make me, Hafu" Tam said in a threatening tone.

"Can you please just let me get pass by, so I can sit down?"

"No, sit on the floor like a dog, Woof, woof!" Tam mocks.

The whole bus is laughing and pointing fingers at me. I am getting embarrass and turn red.

"Seriously, let me go." I said assertively.

"Sit like a good dog or I will make you sit. Be a good boy and obey your master's commands." Tam said in a scornfully fashion,

"Dude, I am not an animal. Tam, let me through."

"What a bad dog! I don't like dogs who disobey their master. Time to put you to sleep."

Tam clenches his fist and throws a haymaker. For some odd reason, I see the punch in slow motion. My reaction time and senses are sublime, and I dodge his fatal punch. The laughter on the bus diminishes into silence.

"Huh?" said Tam.

"Seriously, let me go to my seat."

"How the hell did you…"

Tam swings a sucker-punch but this time, I grab his bare knuckles midway through his punch. The whole bus is astonished in amazement.

"Let me go, Hafu!" whines Tam.

"I won't let you go until you call me by my name." I said.

"Hafu, Hafu…" Tam mocks me again.

I squeeze his fist and Tam cries like a baby. Tears are trickling down Tam's face.

"Ahhhhhh!" cries Tam.

"Say my name."

"Fuck you."

"Say my name, my real name. Give me the respect that I deserve. Don't call me Hafu again."

"Ok, ok! Ahhhh! Kenji! I am sorry." screams Tam.

I let go his hand and Tam let me pass through the aisle. All my classmates had their jaws dropping down to the ground in shock including

Amaya. In a nonchalant fashion, I sit down next to Amaya and I see Mr. Zaki boarding the bus.

"What's all the commotion!" said Mr. Zaki.

"Nothing sir. "said Tam in docile tone.

"Ok, everyone time to go home and keep your conversations at an appropriate volume. "said Mr. Zaki.

The bus drives off onto the road. I am sitting with Amaya and I'm meticulously thinking about what to say to her. It's conspicuous but I am extremely shy, and my father's transferred knowledge didn't help my conversations skills with girls. Like a hurricane, I keep brainstorming ideas in my mind, but I didn't want to come off nerdy or cocky. "Did you see what I did to Tam?" Nope, sounds too egotistical. "You are beautiful." Too cliché. "Want to date me?" too forward. Amaya breaks the ice and says something first.

"What you did to Tam was very E-P-I-C! I can't believe you did that! I am happy that someone put that egomaniac in his place. Where did you learn how to defend yourself like that? It's remarkable! "said Amaya.

"I learned from my father." I said with confidence.

"The one who is deceased?" she asks.

"Yes, he was my great mentor. My dad was in the military."

"Can you show me how to do that?"

"Yes, I can."

We chatted throughout the long duration of the ride about everything from school to family. It felt natural and easy. She keeps asking questions about me and seem very sincere about getting to know who I am. As we arrive to our school and exiting the bus, Amaya holds my hand.

"Ok, I am going to be straight forward with you, Kenji. I like you a lot." Amaya said. "I'll take you home. I have my limo coming around the block to pick us up."

I am surprise about her honesty but simultaneously, I am ecstatic that the feelings are mutual.

"I like you too, Amaya. Ok, I'll take up for the ride."

We chat more in the limousine and share some funny conservations over soda pop. We keep giggling throughout the whole ride. The limousine approaches to my house and stops in the driveway.

"I had a good time with you, Kenji. This doesn't count as our first date. Take my phone number. This is my private secondary phone that my parents do not know about. Text me." said Amaya.

"You have two phones? Nice to be you, Amaya. Ok, I will text you my number. "I said.

"I will get your number when you text me first, silly!"

I begin to blush, and she reaches over to kiss me on the cheek. My cheek tingles and I become immediately mesmerize from it. I open the limousine door and exit the vehicle.

"Ok, I will see you soon Kenji. We need to hangout more. "said Amaya through the half-closed tinted window.

"I agree to that! Once again, thank you for the ride and giving me that awesome bike. I am very appreciative of your kind gesture."

"Don't worry about. Take care, Kenji. Can I call you Ken?"

"Call me whatever you want." I said.

"Ha-ha-ha, ok Ken. Have a good night."

Is this real? Do I have a girlfriend? What a long and crazy day! First, I almost meet death, then I meet my father, turned into a God, make Tam feel inferior, and get a girlfriend? That's what you call a perfect day.

"Hey, Kenji. Come inside the house." said Grandpa.

"What do you need Grandpa?"

"Clean the front porch, kitchen, and your filthy bedroom now!"

"Can I get some sleep first? I am tired."

"After you're done your chores."

"Why do you work me to death?"

"Do it now!"

With the new powers and attributes, chores were child's play. I complete all my chores in five minutes. The Allonian speed is incredible! I swept the front porch, wipe down the kitchen spotless, and my bedroom looks like a five-star hotel room. I told my Grandpa that I finished my chores and he didn't believe me.

"That was only five minutes, you are lying Kenji!" said Grandpa.

"Check it yourself! "I said.

Grandpa, in a rare moment, is speechless.

"How in the hell did you do this?"

I had to make some fib up.

"I learned time management. Six Sigma course at Jen High. I managed to get chores done at an efficient rate."

"I guess you're not as dumb and useless after all. I must see you the next time you clean. I will teach the Samurai ways first thing tomorrow. No chores for you."

"Really?"

"I must teach you how to fight. I don't want you to get bullied again."

"It's okay, I put that jerk Tam in his place."

"Tam is just a teenager and a punk. I am talking about within life. There will be a time where you must shield yourself and to those you love. Men must learn to protect their families and property. The weak are meat; the strong eat. You will appreciate this lesson. It's about discipline and mental strength. I will teach you what my father taught me, which is Kenjutsu. Follow me."

I follow Grandpa throughout the house, and he led me to this a door that I never knew existed. It's a brown door with Japanese writing which means "Meijii". It had a padlock on the knob and Grandpa whips out an ancient and decaying bronze key to open the door.

"This is my dojo. We will train here 4:30 every morning. You are ready. Here take this." said Grandpa.

He gives me spare key for the dojo. This is a humbling experience. I am happy to get inside the sacred dojo but also, it is the first time that feel Grandpa's approval. I don't know if his teachings will be helpful but it's an opportunity to bond with him.

"Thanks, Grandpa. I will be there."

"Be there on time. No excuses."

"Yes sir."

"Go to bed, it's 9:00 PM. You need your shut-eye for energy tomorrow."

"Goodnight, Grandpa."

Night begins to fall and I head to my bedroom for some shut eye. However, I am feeling fairly restless so I decide to stay up a little later than usual. Too many thoughts were swirling in my head after learning about my father's true identity. The medallion is on my desk and I want to test out the Warrior suit. My room is on the first floor so escaping my room is not difficult. I hop out the window and gallop into the fields. I place the medallion on my chest and press the symbol. Nothing happens.

I squeeze the medallion, nothing happens. I get frustrated and stomp on the medallion, nothing happens.

"How the hell do you activate this thing?" I yell.

I start thinking and tap in my transferred knowledge. A lightbulb turned on.

"Duh, turn the medallion over. I had it backwards."

Once again, I press the symbol, spin the medallion into the correct position and placed it on my chest. Suddenly, the medallion latch on my chest tightly and silver steel leaks out which wraps around my body. My arms, hands, and legs become metallic. The steel surrounds my face to form a mask and helmet. The helmet has a v-shaped crescent. The plasma sword places on my waist. Large wings begin to manifest onto my back. I felt the compelling energy throughout my body. My suit becomes complete and I feel invincible!

It's time to test out this Warrior suit. I bend on one knee, place both hands on the ground and blast off like a rocket towards the stratosphere. Flying is the ultimate freedom especially zipping through the clouds. Miraculously, I manage to avoid some airplanes which could have been a potential disaster. As I am flying towards the o-zone layer, I feel the pressure but not the heat. As I enter outer space, I see Earth from an uncommon view. My eyes widen as I gaze upon the beautiful spectacle of Earth. Impeccable time for a selfie! As I am enjoying the sights of Earth from space, a floating asteroid comes into my direction. I put my hands together like a diamond and blast the asteroid into smithereens. The power is outstanding! First time in my life, I feel like a God.

The confidence begins to engulf me, and it is borderline cocky. No hesitation, I fly back to Earth towards the Sahara Desert. I see wild camels rambling and sand dunes surrounding the area. The forces from my flight causes a sandstorm as I zoom by. Next stop is the United States of America and see the Statue of Liberty. Her crown becomes my landing pad as I take a moment to see the breathtaking view of the city that never sleeps, New York City. Never experiencing a New York City pizza before, I decide to grab a slice. I travel to the top of the Empire State Building, take off the suit, zoom through the stairs, and make my way into Manhattan. There is a pizzeria *name Lalo's Pizza* and I order a pepperoni slice with extra cheese to go. There's a dark alley and I head there to transform into the Warrior suit for flight mode. Back in the air, I fly to Paris, the city of lights and love. The Eiffel Tower is standing strong as I fly circles around it. Heading East, I check out the Wall of the China. The path is long and well crafted. There are unlimited bricks and steps which makes me appreciate the human architect and design. Before heading home, I fly south to Australia to land in Sydney, Australia. I have plenty of room in stomach for more food, so I order an Angus burger with some extra ketchup. The burger is juicy and flavorful. I fly back to Japan and realizing that globetrotting is an awesome experience.

Before heading back to home, I had a mission to accomplish. I call it "OPERATION: END THE TAM. Tam did apologize on the bus during the trip, which is uncharacteristic for him, but his wicked ways need to be obsolete. Tam almost took my life away at Mount Tenchi and he is a threat to others at Jen High. His money and power will embolden him to continue to be a power-hungry demon towards others. It's time to end Tam Hideki.

Quietly, I glide into Tari and land on Tam's Estate which is gigantic and gaudy. The mansion is gratuitously enormous and lavish with marble stairs and gold rails. The driveway is about a mile long with multiple huge water foundations splashing in unison. There are statues of his father, mother, and him all over the property. The Hideki's are very narcissistic which explains Tam's egocentric and psychopathic behavior. The house is heavily secured with numerous cameras and security guards. Lasers are also on the ground to cause an alarm to go off.

To avoid the guards and security devices, I put Warrior suit into incognito mode which makes me invisible. Calmly, I hover through the property and notice Tam's bedroom window is open. Without a peep, I sneak in his room and he's snoring very loudly. He's cuddling with a fuzzy teddy bear and I cover my mouth from giggling. In jest, I gave him a nudge to wake up.

"Hey, I am trying to sleep. Leave me alone…. what the hell!"

Tam screams like an eight-year-old girl.

"Ahhh!!!!!!!"

"I am the Metallic Samurai. Come with me, now!" I said.

"I don't want to, where's my mommy?" cries Tam.

With no mercy, I intensely grip Tam's arm and take him onto an exquisite flight out the window. We are hovering 1,000 feet in the air and Tam is crying hysterically. We fly over the city of Tokyo and traffic below is heavy and aggressive. I flip Tam upside down, drew my plasma sword, and point the plasma blade towards his neck.

"Put me down! Put me down!" pleads Tam.

"I will put you down when you leave Kenji Jackson alone!" I said.

"Ok, I will." Tam agrees.

"You speak with Principal Wong, admit your wrongs, and do not treat Kenji and others like that again." I said sternly.

"Yes, yes, please put me down. I am sorry! I was a bad boy, no more."

"Are you sure you want to be put down, I can let you splatter in the traffic down there!"

"Oh, god no! I want to live! Please no!"

"You will not terrorize people ever again. You will not marginalize a person in a disadvantage place in society. You will take your money and give back to the community, not for evil deeds that fulfill your twisted fantasies. If you do, you will die! Do you understand my message?"

"Yes, Metal Samurai! Please forgive me!"

I notice that Tam is urinating his pants and for some reason, I had compassion for him. Killing Tam is not in the plans due my good nature. Implementing fear in his heart for the first time in his spoil and privileged life is the ultimate goal. Great way to accomplish that is to drop him in the middle of Tokyo towards the traffic.

"Ahhhhhhhhhhhh!"

Then, I swoop down to grab Tam right before he hit the pavement.

"This is just a warning. Next time, it's death! Change your ways. Be more." I said firmly.

"Yes, Metal Samurai, I will be a good boy. You will see." Tam said in a childlike matter.

"Get out of my sight you cretin, now!"

"Ahhhhhhhh!"

Tam runs away in panic down the sidewalk and disappears in the city. My mission is complete. I fly back to home, but it is late. It is 3:30 AM but some reason, I couldn't sleep. My adrenaline is running on cloud nine and I can't stop thinking the possibilities from this Warrior suit.

Instead of taking a catnap, I go to the dojo an hour early for meditation. Grandpa is in the dojo with hot green tea.

"Before we train, we drink tea. I am surprise that you are thirty minutes early." said Grandpa.

"I couldn't sleep. I am ready to learn your wisdom." I said.

"I am pleased that you are, now drink."

The tea is very potent. It risen my alertness and cognitive levels.

"We begin to train. Put this on." said Grandpa.

Grandpa gives me a Hakama to wear and hands me a well-honed katana for the *Kenjutsu* training. The swordsmanship of a samurai is an art form. I pick up the *Kenjutsu* very swiftly and Grandpa is surprisingly intrigue by my progress.

"You're picking *Kenjutsu* extremely fast. Just be more patient but you have a good grasp of it."

Grandpa is very well balanced and fluent with his *Kenjutsu*. I saw the passion in his eyes. From this point on, I will let go all my resentment for my Grandpa. He's a proud Japanese man that loves his history, culture, and family legacy. It took some time but he's opening his heart to his grandson.

We finish the session about 6:00 and I had to leave for school. I told Grandpa that I love the teachings and he is smiling ear to ear.

"We will do this every other day." said Grandpa. "Chores need to be done. Have a good day."

"Thanks Grandpa."

I told my mother goodbye and head for school. Instead of riding my bike, I put on my Warrior suit and flew to Jen High which took only 30 seconds. No more bike riding which is fantastic! First class flights on KENJI AIR will be the norm. Quietly, I land on the school's roof and change into my school uniform. There's a set of stairs which I take it down to the first floor. The bell rings, and it is Japanese History class. Mr. Zaki produces a pop-quiz and for the first time, I am ready for it. The test is in Japanese and I can read it with ease. My penmanship becomes impeccable and I am able to answer the questions with depth, critically thinking, and detail. I finish the quiz in sixty seconds and Mr. Zaki becomes suspicious.

"There's no way that you finish the quiz. There is fifteen questions and it should take you twenty minutes to complete." said Mr. Zaki.

"No, I am done. "I said.

Mr. Zaki checks the quiz and his eyes lit up in astonishment.

"Amazing! Every answer is correct. This is high quality work. Doctoral level!" said Mr. Zaki.

"Thanks!" I said.

The rest of class stop their pencils to stare at me. They are probably thinking, "How did this idiot go from barely making the grades to top of the class"?

The next class is physical education and I become a gym class hero. My athleticism increases by 1000%. We are playing basketball and I score a quadruple double. 97 points, 67 rebounds, 76 assists, and 55 blocks. The students couldn't handle my 360 dunks or crossovers. Mr. Yugo, the P.E. teacher, shakes my hand and ask me to join the basketball team.

The final class is physics which is the toughest course in the school. It's mandatory and if you don't pass, you are automatically expelled from Jen High. Mrs. Hinata is the meanest teacher in Jen High, and she doesn't take any crap from anyone. If you are a minute late, you get points taken off. If you fall asleep, she will give you extra work. Mrs. Hinata tests are tremendously rigid. Do not forget the date in the right corner. If you forget that part, automatic failure. Trust me, I know because she fails me twice because I didn't write the date in YYYY/MM/DD format. The lady is certified looney. Usually, I get anxious and begin to perspire like soda can on a hot day when I walk in her class but this time, I am poise.

"Test time, you have thirty minutes to complete packet. Mr. Jackson you have sixty minutes since you are struggling in my class." said Mrs. Hinata.

Right on cue, the whole class laughs at me, but I didn't care. She drops the packet and there were two hundred questions which is complete insanity. I mark the date on the right corner, and I complete the test in record-breaking three minutes. It could've been one minute, but I took the leisure to stare at Amaya's beauty for a moment. With confidence, I stand up and hand in my test packet. Mrs. Hinata becomes antagonistic.

"You are not done. No pupil at Jen High can finish my test within five minutes. You did it in three minutes which means either you quit, or you are pulling my leg. Jokes aren't tolerated in my class. Finish your packet or fail." said Mrs. Hinata.

"I am done. Check the work. I also added new methods to calculate kinetic energy. "I reply.

She opens the packet and becomes shock in disbelief.

"Every answer is correct! This does not add up. You barely pass the test before, suddenly you are Stephen Hawking? Go to the Principal Wong's office, now!" yells Mrs. Hinata.

"Why? I did the work! Check it. All original algorithms."

"Go or you fail my class."

With some smugness, I go to Principal Wong's office. Mrs. Hinata is inside the office whining about how I cheated her Physics test and wants me to redo the packet. She also wants me to conduct the test in front of Principal Wong.

"You will do the test after school today. I see that you ace Mr. Zaki's history class with doctoral level responses. Impressive but suspicious. Then, you pass Mrs. Hinata's test with 100% accuracy which makes you only student to receive this grade in Jen High's history. You are a struggling student who barely passes school but now you're a prodigy whiz-kid? In my thirty years being the principal of this prestigious school, I have never heard or seen a student of your caliber improved this vastly which brings major red flags and suspicion. You will retake this test and I will watch your every move." said Principal Wong.

"That's unfair. I completed the test and I passed it."

"I don't care what's fair. I am the Principal here. You will retake this test or be expelled."

"Let's make a deal. If I fail, I will leave for good. If I pass, you will write me a letter of recommendation for college."

"Is that right? I will write the letter right after you complete the test. Don't get too cocky."

"Let me do the test right now!" I said with assertion.

"Ok, fine. Mrs. Hinata give this arrogant punk the packet." said Principal Wong.

"Here you go, Kenji. This is the "B" version of the test with additional 250 Physic questions. It's the most difficult test that I assembled. You will have only thirty minutes to complete it."

"It seems like you want me to fail but ok, whatever." I said.

"You are over-confident." Mrs. Hinata.

"Hand me the test lady!" I said with a condescending attitude.

"My word, you are rude. Here you go. This will be your final test at Jen High."

I begin the test and it is ridiculously simple to me. Numbers and formulas were second nature due to my enhanced Allonian intelligence. I completed the test in two minutes as Principal Wong and Mrs. Hinata were silent in confusion and disbelief.

"It's complete. Check the work." I said.

Mrs. Hinata checks every page with her answer key. She is speechless.

"Well, Mrs. Hinata did he pass or fail? "said Principal Wong.

"Every answer is correct. I am humbling myself to say……. Kenji Jackson is a living mastermind prodigy that's beyond our comprehension. I sincerely apologize for not believing your craft. I don't know what happen, but you tap into a level that surpasses me. I will recommend Kenji Jackson to MIT. My brother is the president there and I want you to be in his school."

"Thank you, Mrs. Hinata. I will think about that offer and I will accept your apology. I think you have a letter to write. Here's a pen Principal Wong." I said.

"Errr…." said Principal Wong as he eats crow.

"Am I dismissed?" I said.

"Yes, Kenji. Have a pleasant day. Your letter will be mailed tomorrow. Give me your address." said Principal Wong.

Victorious! I give him my address and place it on Principal Wong's desk. Principal Wong extends his arm for a handshake and I extend my arm as well. No words were exchange but I detect a mutual respect. Tam bursts in the office with paranoia while wearing his pajamas from last night.

"Principal Wong!" said Tam.

"Why aren't you in uniform? "said Principal Wong.

"Long story sir. I must say something that is very imperative. Kenji Jackson is a good student and person. Please don't reprimand him about the fight. It was my culpability, "said Tam with contrition." I threw Kenji's bicycle in the street which caused the scuffle. Kenji is my friend and I want fully to apologize to him and you for not acting as a Jen High gentleman. I want to donate $100,000 for a scholarship to Kenji towards any school that he desires."

"Wow, that's very admirable. Your honesty shows integrity. Ok, Kenji. No detention or extra work. You're no longer on probation for expulsion. However, the $100,000 donation must be processed properly with the Jen High Alumni Association. Speak with our representatives for the donation. Kenji, you're a blessed young man. Your friend Tam is giving you a bright future. You should thank him for his generous offer. But please Mr. Hideki, put your uniform on. If you need extra shirts, pants, and quarters, go to the next room." said Principal Wong.

"I want to say thank you for the generous offer, but I must reject it. I want to thank you for being honest about the incident, but I want you to be kinder to people and treat them with dignity. I will earn my education, no handouts. For many years, I survived by standing on my own two feet. My father taught me to have self-reliance and tenacity. Life isn't fair, but I can't dwell upon the unfairness. Through these harsh experiences, I became a resilient person. Thanks, Tam, for the offer, but I respectfully must say no. I will get an academic scholarship based upon merit. Have a good day Principal Wong and Tam."

With full pride, I walk out the office and for the first time, I felt respected. However, I begin to ponder, is respect based upon fear? Does fear make others respect you? Fear isn't the right path to earn respect. I just wanted to be respected as a person, but some people don't see respect that way. Tam Hideki thought fear is respect which is why he continue to be a tyrant towards me. Mrs. Hinata wanted students to fear by creating a rigid curriculum. Principal Wong constantly used threats and scare tactics to "keep me in line". Fear is just an illusion of respect. My only wish is to be free from provocation. However, I can't lie. Being feared feels somewhat good.

This brings me to my conclusion about Nefaric. King Saloh didn't respect him and never loved him as much as Candor. Resentment manifested, and hell brewed inside Nefaric's heart. Aggression and force are his tactics to generate fear into the illusion of respect. Nefaric knew that he can't surpass my father's status no matter how hard he tried to win over his King Saloh's approval. Nefaric also came to realization that he can't defeat Candor one on one. Candor's intelligence intimidates Nefaric. But how come he didn't show up to Earth to retrieve the medallion at an earlier time? That's puzzling to me. I know that Nefaric is coming and I must prepare for his arrival. Whenever that is….

CHAPTER 6

NEFARIC TOUCHES EARTH

After my transformation, my life is so much sweeter. For the first time, I am on the honor roll time at Jen High. Nothing is a greater feeling than that except I have Amaya as my main squeeze. Due to my skills in gym class heroics, I am named the newest captain on the basketball team. Principal Wong honor his promise with the recommendation letter. Instead of mailing the letter, he comes to my house and spoke to my mother and Grandpa. My mother cries with joy and gives Principal Wong a big hug. Grandpa seems flabbergasted that his grandson is doing great in school.

"You should be proud of Kenji. He exemplifies what it means to be a pupil at Jen High. "said Principal Wong.

"Thank you, sir." I said.

Mount Tenchi is calling my name and go back into the cave to learn more from my father. Though he is in the Galactic realm, I feel like he is alive. I inform him about the ions which I didn't find the energy to revive Alloy and the other planets. He keeps encouraging me to be patient and expand my mind. My father is my rock that keeps me humble and focus.

Now that I can create silver steel with my bare hands, I am official an entrepreneur. My mother works too much and I want to help her with the financial burdens. Overnight, I design an online store and phone applications with a catchy store, "Silver Dreams". Customized and repairing jewelry is my new side hobby which help my mother with the bills. My mother thinks that I am working as a waiter but she does not know about my secret side business. Within a month, I made over 500,000 yen per day! Also, I finished a beautiful necklace for Amaya using her name in full platinum which is worth a million dollars and I'm planning to give it to her after my championship basketball tournament.

Being the captain on the basketball team made me exceedingly popular overnight. Basketball change me from regular student, to a superstar. Every single day, students and teachers are asking me for autographs. Sometimes, the local news station will ask for interviews at my school. The student body coins me a new nickname which is "K-Dog". The new inherited popularity occasionally makes Amaya very insecure because other ladies were calling my name from the bleachers. "Kenji", "Kenji" when I step on basketball court. My talent is sublime, and I make every shot, free throw, and dunk on the basketball court and led my Jen High Lions to the championship to play Valor High which is in Tokyo. Valor High is our rival school and we are playing in Tokyo for all the marbles. In past years, Jen High never defeated Valor High in school history and pressure to succeed is enormous. The team had many athletes that could go professional. My team did not have those caliber players, they stink! However, I am their only hope and I have to play like a God to win…. wait as second…. I am God!

We get to Valor High and their fans are rowdy and ruthless. Valor High fans are throwing paper balls at our team's heads as we enter the basketball court. There are posters with my name on it saying "Kenji Sucks" or "Jen High Stinks". It is an intimidating environment, but I thrive on moments like this. Amaya is in the stands cheering me on and I want to put on a show for her. Time to tuck in my jersey and head half court for the tipoff.

Referees blow the whistle and tosses the basketball in the air. I grab the rebound and dribble down the court. I am facing the best basketball player in Japan named Shinta Goya. He is 6'7 and plays with a militant and brash attitude. His signature move is the fade-away hook-shot which is obtuse but efficient. Shinta tries to steal the ball away from me but I did a spin move to evade his defense. I hop on one foot and dunk from the free-throw line. Jen High fans went crazy with enthusiasm while the Valor High fans were in shock. Shinta attempts his famous signature hook shot but I block the ball into the stands. Throughout the game, my defense shuts down all five positions on the hardwood. The center could not rebound, the point guard couldn't get pass half court, the small forward couldn't get open, power forward is confused, and Shinta couldn't make a basket. I scored 132 points, 50 steals, 70 blocks and 85 rebounds. The only reason Valor score any points is because my coach benches me in the 3rd quarter due to the landslide point margin. Final Score: 167-21 and Jen High decisively achieves glory against our nemesis. Shinta Goya jogs over to me to shakes my hand which he utters "you are a legend." Mother and Grandpa in the stands and give them a hug.

"You did it son!" said Mom.

"You are simply amazing, Kenji" said Grandpa.

"I wish your father were here to see this. "said Mom

"Yeah, he's always there in my heart, Mom. "I said

Amaya jumps on back and kisses me on the cheek.

"Babe, you were unreal out there!" said Amaya.

"Amaya, I want to show you something." I said.

"What is it?"

"Here, I made this for you."

"Wow, this is a beautiful necklace! It is very shiny! Thank you, Kenji! I love you so much!"

"Hey, Kenji! Are you going to kiss your girl all night or hang with the fellas!" said Coach Yugo.

"Amaya, I gotta go. We will see each other later." I said.

"Ok, you deserve it. Have fun champ!" said Amaya.

I celebrate with the team and we pop non-alcoholic sparkling cider in the locker room. We were jumping with joy and dancing in victory.

"I am proud of you boys. I want to thank our captain Kenji for joining the team. This is the happiest day of my life. We never defeated Valor High…. NEVER! We did it fellas, we did it! I am proud of every one of you. Let us take this trophy and celebrate tonight and tomorrow at school!"

We high five and head onto the team bus. As the bus took off the road, something did not feel right. I am feeling some premonition and it is not a positive energy. I sense an evil and powerful energy. Is it Nefaric? Apprehension is circuiting my mind.

"What's wrong, Kenji?" said my teammate Trey Udoki. "Sing with us bro!"

The whole team is singing the Jen High Alma Mater and I sing along with them. It temporarily keeps my mind off that feeling but I could not just shake off the feeling entirely. Something wicked is prone to happen.

The next day, Jen High honors the basketball during a pep rally inside our basketball arena. Principal Wong is standing full of pride from a podium and delivers an honorary speech to the team.

"Coach Yugo, and the Jen High Lions. I want to thank you for bringing in the championship for our prestigious school. We waited over 89 years to bring glory back to our campus. I was on the basketball team in 1968 and we were never close to beating that juggernaut. We are blessed to have Kenji Jackson as a pupil at Jen High and I want to award him the highest honor. The Scarlet Kimono."

Principal hands me the kimono and it has my name on the back with Japanese lettering. I felt really proud and the crowd commence a standing ovation. While everyone is happy and giving me an abundance of appreciation, that evil premonition comes back to me. I see Mr. Zaki running onto the stage to inform Principal Wong a message. It did not seem favorable or positive. Principal Wong's changes from proud to despair.

"Ladies and gentlemen, we are being attacked!" said Principal Wong. "There is terrorism in Tokyo. We must go! Stay calm and leave Jen High in an orderly fashion."

"What's going on Principal Wong?" I ask.

"We have to go, Kenji."

The faculty and students enters into panic mode. Screams echo the arena and fear is ubiquitous. My cell phone notifications are ringing and buzzing in my front denim pocket. While checking my phone, I see a text message from the local news. "Tokyo under attack! Find shelter!" There are video clips attach to the message displaying multiple UFOs hovering the city. Lasers and bombs are being discharge from the UFOs. One of the UFOs lands in the middle of Tokyo and thousands of aliens deploy into the streets. The aliens are Allonians as I recognize the insignias on their uniforms. Tokyo Police and military are battling the Allonians, but it seems futile. Tokyo citizens are running rampant in fright trying to survive the annihilation. There is a live feed on my news application and I switch over to see the real time events. The news is streaming from their helicopter to record the action from the skies. There he is…. Nefaric. He slowly hovers from his spaceship with his red metallic armor. Eerily, he looks exactly like my father but slightly more built in stature. Suddenly, Nefaric flies up to the news sky-cam and yells in Allonians which translated "where is Kenji!" Nefaric draws a plasma sword and destroys the helicopter. The live feed disappears, and I drop the phone in disbelief. What should I do? I do not feel ready and shaking in my bones. Adrenaline is rushing to my head and I know I must act.

"Kenji, what's happening? I am scared." said Amaya.

"Don't be. Just stay home. I have to leave." I said.

"Ok, I'll take you home."

"No, I am going somewhere else…"

"Where? Kenji!!!"

Amaya must not know my whereabouts. I run in the hallway and out the backdoor behind the school. I hide behind a smelly green dumpster and transform into the Warrior-suit. Time to turn on flight mode and head to Tokyo.

As I glide through the air, I see pure obliteration. Skyscrapers are tumbling into ruins, asphalt from the streets are deteriorating, vehicles are on fire or flipped upside down, soldiers are injured or dead, and a proliferation of destruction reigning profoundly in the city. I see Nefaric directly his soldiers to destroy more of Tokyo. I fly down and start to shout.

"NEFARIC! STOP!" I shout.

Nefaric speaks in Allonian

"Tiyo Heppa Boolu Cas Ta Beya (My soldiers, cease fire now)" said Nefaric.

The Allonian soldiers cease their assault. I land right in front of Nefaric. He is intimidating and possess reddish-green eyes. Suddenly, he speaks again.

"Falo, malo (My nephew) You are Candor's son" said Nefaric.

"Yes, I am. I know why you are here and there is no need to kill these innocent people. If you want to fight, then it's me!" I said with anger.

"You're assuming too much. Settle down, nephew. "said Nefaric. "Interesting, you sort of look like me. Strong Allonian traits."

Nefaric raises his arm and expands his hand. Nervousness sets in and accidently, I shoot a glove blast directly towards Nefaric. However, Nefaric deflects my beam with ease into the air which explodes like fireworks."

"How did you block my attack?" I said.

"You need to work on your attack, very amateurish. Why are you so hostile? Is this how you treat your Uncle? Relax, Kenji. I am not attacking you, be calm. I am reading your mind."

Nefaric extends his arm with his palm open. He closes his eyes and meditates. Unexpectedly, he opens his eyes.

"Ah, ha!" said Nefaric.

"What did you do?" I ask.

"I analyzed your past. The shame and pain that you endured. Similar to my circumstances. You never were accepted into society. We are more identical than you know."

"No, I am not. I am not a murderer like you. You killed my father!"

"Hmm..indeed, I did. I must admit but it was necessary. Your father is a man with no integrity. Left Alloy into ruins because he hid the truth from the people. Your father Candor only cared about himself and impressing my father, King Saloh. I am here to restore Alloy and retrieve the medallion back for the restoration for our planet."

"No, you want it for control and power. I will not give it to you."

"Ha, ha! You are a stubborn one. It is an Allonian trait. I think your father didn't do a good job explaining what your purpose is and shall show you."

Nefaric shoots an energy beam and it is impossible to dodge it. I attempt to avoid but it is a direct hit. However, I did not feel any pain and I transport into a different realm. It is pitch black, no ground yet I am standing firmly. A bright light blinds my pupils and Nefaric appears.

"Where the hell are we?" I said.

"This is conscience. We are inside your mind." Nefaric replies.

"My mind?" I said

"Yes, I am in the conscience. Remember Captain Derkins?" Nefaric replies in arrogance.

"How do you know about him? What about Captain Derkins, he was my father's best friend."

"Captain Derkins was one of my soldiers who spied on Candor. Captain Derkins is Lieutenant Major Barium, second highest rank soldier and Chief of Espionage. We generated a camouflage to suppress his Allonian energy and went undercover for intel on Candor. Lt. Major Barium communicated the calculations to our chief of staff and we executed the Chemo-Lightening. As a soldier, I would have ripped Candor into fragments but due to his dangerous behavior and erratic tactics, we delivered the weapon from a distance. As Candor was navigating that primitive aircraft, Lt. Major Barium deliver the location and mission complete. Candor is very capable to make a new medallion. Eliminating him means, no more production of medallions. We thought the medallion disappeared from the Chemo-Lightning attack, but your recent activation alarmed our intel. We want to demolish the medallion for good. No one should have this power. I do not want Radium or Gallium to have it. Please, give it to me."

"Never! You killed my father! I should kill you now! I am not that foolish to give you this power for you to utilize it for tyranny."

"Settle down, young lad. I realize that you suffered in an abundance during childhood and adolescents. I sincerely apologize if you were dejected from your father's demise, but he put Alloy's future at risk. I did not have any indication that Candor had a child until the medallion became activated which sent a signal back to Alloy hence why I am here on this unusual planet. Kenji, my nephew, I am sorry that I took Candor's life, but I did what was necessary and what Allonians are born to do which is to protect the mother planet. Candor caused confusion and mischief. His invention of the AFOP was more of a burden than a blessing. Candor may have had good intentions for Alloy, but he cultivated hostility and imbalance amongst the planets. Gallium and Radium provoked a war towards Alloy, killed our people, and we cease fire? The lives that were taken due to secrecy and deceit, would want that in a future King? Be honest, is that what you want as a leader? The truth aches and it is not pleasant to devour but it must be told. Your father is not the great man you think he is, he's an embarrassment to the Allonian gods!

Kenji, he left your life in ruins. Candor put you on this planet to become a mediocre human. You had to endure hatred from these people, oppression, and humiliation. They called you…what is it… "Hafu"? Isn't that a derogatory statement to shun you? You were heavily marginalized into something insignificant which is disheartening. These people did not accept you as a human, do you think they will accept you as an Allonian? They will not!

Return to Alloy with me and be King! Our planet is in war and we need to restore Alloy now. You must give me the medallion and come with me to Alloy to help our legacy. You are the King Kenji, take your place as the leader of the Allonians!"

"King?"

"Yes, King Kenji. Become the Allonian that you were destined to be. Take the reins. I will give you until the fortnight. I know this is an overwhelming load of information to comprehend. This is life altering for you. Kenji, I will give enough duration to reflect about your destiny. I will return Alloy and come back to this planet with your decision…..... Soldiers! Retreat to your ships at once!"

"Yes, my lord!" said the Allonian soldiers.

"I shall return…."

The ships ascended into the atmosphere in a flash and I become numb with confusion. As much as I want to obliterate Nefaric, the one man that killed my father, he possess some valid points. Why should I be on this planet for? This land gave me hell for years. My grandfather treats me like crap because I am half-black. The school did not accept me because I didn't come from a privileged background and not fully Japanese. Why should I care? Would Amaya give me a chance if it weren't for my enhance abilities? I do not think so. My life is a blatant lie. My father's missteps caused three planets to have a war. His mistakes caused my life hell and he is not honest with me in the beginning of my life. Candor is a genius with creation of planets and AFOP but his actions caused more harm than good. I do not know how to feel. The truth is exceedingly difficult to digest. I can see both sides of moon. The utilitarianism in me understands Nefaric's logic. As cruel as murdering your own brother, Nefaric thinks he is doing what is right for the greater good. However, why murder? Your own brother? I do not know how to feel.

"Put your hands in the air, now!" yells a policeman.

Japanese police and military point their weapons at me. Before the police and military were about to pull the triggers, I go into incognito and hover away. In full speed, I fly away towards Mount Tenchi. Time to talk to my father. I start pondering. Should I leave Earth for Alloy?

CHAPTER 7

RETRIEVE THE IONS

"Why did you invent the AFOP and keep it in secrecy?" I said.

"It's for the greater good for Alloy. If I revealed the power to all three planets than it would have fallen unto the wrong hands. It was meant for good and I didn't want the energy to convert into something wicked." said Father.

"It caused war for three planets. Allonians died over the energy you invented. Ultimately, it took your life away. It is your fault, father! You let me suffer your ten years in Japan. My life is a sham!"

"Kenji, I can't change the past, but you have the power to change the present for the future. Kenji, do not believe the twisted lies from Nefaric. He is getting to your head. Psychological warfare is his strength. He knows how to galvanize the troops and inspiring his men and women to fight for him. This is a strategic tactic to get the medallion. He doesn't care about you; he wants you to perish. Mainly, due to the fact you are an extension of me. A threat to his throne."

"He told me that I can be King and save Alloy from destruction. That does not sound like a man that feels threatened. Nefaric comes across as reassuring."

"I can't believe what I am hearing, Kenji! Nefaric is brainwashing you! Remember son, he killed me in the most cowardly way. Do not be naïve. You will never be King as long Nefaric is still alive. Nefaric is taking advantage of your vulnerable emotions. He is using your anquish as leverage against me. The AFOP is the best invention for Alloy. It facilitated the entire planet to full efficiency. The point of discretion for the AFOP is to protect the integrity of the energy for the purpose of good. Nefaric will use it for destruction and oppress the people of Radium and Gallium hence why he was excluded from the AFOP Act. I know my brother and your uncle. Nefaric craves power, something he never had before which is why he overthrown the Alloy Kingdom."

"You may invent the AFOP but it really affected Alloy. Thousands of Allonians perished over it. You died over it. It's too much power for one god to obtain."

"No, it's not. Kenji, please listen to me. Do not fall for Nefaric's persuasion. That medallion is designed for the worthy Allonians, not him. My brother was never worthy. No Allonian would attack another Allonian without a justifiable cause. Nefaric is pure evil, do not let him have the medallion."

"Why should I protect Earth? This place has been hell for me. These emotional scars don't just go away, Father. It seeps through your soul. Earth is not where I belong anymore. Alloy is my calling. Why should I care?"

"Because Allonians are born to protect those who are weaker than themselves. It is our core values. If Nefaric had the chance to utilize the medallion, he would use it for selfish gain and tyranny. Allonians may be Gods but we are not perfect. We cannot foresee the future. Please forgive me for your rough childhood but you grew up to be a fine young man and I am proud of you. Adversity builds character which you will survive the obstacles of society and remain strong. Listen to me son, I have your best interest at heart. I am your father."

Father's words resonate in my psyche.

"I am sorry for what I said. It was a built-up pain over the years of your absence. I need more time to heal." I said.

"I understand. "said Father" Let me show you the Warrior suit other special features. I meant to mention these other features before, but I did not test them in the experimental phase. These are prototype features that are active for usage."

"Other features?"

"Yes, there's more to the suit than what you know. You can split the plasma sword into two. Press the middle buttons on both side of the *tsuka* simultaneously with your palms. If you spin the swords, it converts into a plasma disc. Original design was for cutting steel on construction projects. You can utilize this as an effective weapon. Test out the duel plasma swords."

As I press the button, the plasma sword splits into two. I spin the swords and it becomes a rotating disc. I throw the disc like a Frisbee towards a large boulder that slices in half with ease.

"That's incredible"

"Another feature is the "steel cannon". It is attached to your wings. Press your shoulders to detach the wings. Put your plasma sword between the wings. There will be a gravitational pull that will from a cannon. The original purpose…well I thought it was a kick-idea."

I followed my father's instructions and the wings of my suit became an ultimate weapon.

"This is awesome!"

"Do not utilize the weapon here in the cave. Go on top of Mount Tenchi."

I reach the top of Mount Tenchi with the steel cannon on hand. Father is there with a gigantic stone.

"I will toss this stone and you will hit the target."

Father tosses the stone about 500 feet in the air. My eye is focus in the scope and I pull the trigger. The kickback is powerful and I stumble a few steps as an enormous plasma beam discharges towards the target. The stone vanishes as the plasma contacts the stone and light from the plasma illuminates the skies.

"This cannon is legit!"

"This is a dangerous weapon. You can use this in few quantities. The cannon may need duration for a recharge once the plasma liquids are exhausted. This is your most powerful weapon at your disposal. You must be very meticulous with the cannon because it does have the power to eradicate planets."

"If I missed, I could've destroyed Earth! Why didn't you tell prior of me shooting it?!?"

"I have trust in you, Kenji. I need to prepare you for the battle against Nefaric. Let us train now."

"Yes, father."

We go back inside Mount Tenchi and father trains me more about the suit. Father teaches me how to dodge energy spheres and beams.

"When a beam comes directly towards you, there's two options: avoid or counter. I will shoot a sphere at you and I want to see your reaction. Ready?"

"Yes, I am ready."

Father gets in an odd stance and all of sudden a green sphere comes at me at a rapid rate. I could not dodge it and the sphere hits me but I didn't feel any pain.

"What happened?"

"Son, you have to be quicker than that. I discharge a placebo sphere that does not contain plasma. It just to test your reflexes. You will not be able to handle sphere attacks if you move to slow. Let us attempt this again. Focus on the objective!"

"Ok, father. Let's do it."

My father gets in that grotesque stance once more and shoots another sphere. This time, I focus on the sphere and I am able to reflect the sphere towards the cave ceilings.

"That's it, son! Let's do over and over until you master the art of defense."

"Ok, let's go."

Father discharges hundreds of spheres at a time and I am able to deflect the majority of them. We conducted training for three hours and I became fatigue.

"I am wiped out."

"This is nothing, Kenji. When it comes to battle, you won't have any time to take a breather. Nefaric is a warfighter that romanticizes the concept of battle. He loves the challenge of battle which gives him glory and honor. Nefaric is competitive and loves to win despite rules and regulations.

I will give you an example. On planet Alloy, we have a sport called Allo Ball which somewhat like basketball except it's more physical. There are two baskets on each side, a field that is three hundred yards long, and a ball that weighs four hundred pounds. There are twelve players on both sides and you must score as many baskets within two hours of play. Points were worth five points each and tackling is part of the game. Nefaric is a fantastic player in Allo Ball, but not better than me! I am legendary."

"Legendary? Someone is tooting their own horn."

"Yes, I am but I was legendary. My team was called the Comets and his team was called Supernovas. It was a league of eight teams, but the Comets and Supernovas always ended up at the championship."

"Don't mean to cut you off, but how come you didn't play on the same teams?"

"King Saloh didn't want the other Allonians to think we were being favored or receiving bias calls by the referees due to our royalty status. Besides, Nefaric didn't want to be on my team anyways. It was his way to outshine me in front of 700,000 Allonians."

"700,000! That's a huge stadium!"

"It was our coliseum. Many Allonians became injured in this game. You could clothesline a player if they are trying to advance the ball. There wasn't much rules except winning. Nefaric took winning to heart. He doesn't like to lose at any cost.

The game came down to one point. It was tie game 176-176. There was only 2:00 left in the game and the Supernovas had possession. Nefaric dribbles the ball down the field and runs over my teammate. One rule in Allo Ball is that you can run over a player, but you cannot use your shoulder to their face. Nefaric broke the rule which resulted in losing possession:

(In Alloy)

"Hey, that's unfair ref!" said Nefaric. "That's bullshit. He was falling into my shoulder!"

"Rules are the rules Nefaric. Comets ball."

"Are you fucking kidding me!"

"Relax, brother. The game will end very soon after we score the winning shot."

"Shut the hell up, Candor. You have to get passed me."

The referee puts the ball at half-field. The Allonian crowd is roaring with enthusiasm. I call timeout for a strategy.

"Hey, men. We will beat the Supernova. Nefaric is very impatient when it comes to cross the half-field and he will attempt to hit me. I will play decoy and I will throw the ball to Bodago and he will score the game winning basket."

"I don't know if I can do it. I can't catch to save my life," Bodago.

"We all know that Bodago, but this time you will get this catch. That's the plan. To throw out the team, we will throw the ball to an unexpected player. You will be successful. Just go out there and do what I say, everything will fall into place."

"Okay, Candor. I will listen to you. If I drop it, it won't be my fault."

"Believe in yourself, Bodago."

"Yeah, Bodago, just stop worrying about it." said Iahampi.

"Iahampi, just block Nefaric so I can make the pass. Ok, let's do it!"

Iahampi is a large Allonian man who may be the strongest Allonian on the planet. He stands at 6'11 and has muscles larger than tree trunks. His best skill was blocking a defender. As planned, Nefaric rushes to tackle me to cause a fumble. Iahampi shifts in last second and blocks Nefaric's advancement. I throw the ball to Bodago who was wide open, and he made the winning basket. The whole Allo Stadium went into a frenzy and kept cheering "Bodago! Bodago!" Nefaric was despondent and filled with rage.

"I can't believe we lost again! That incompetent referee!"

Nefaric picks the ball and launches it at the referee's head which made him unconscious. I try to calm Nefaric down but punches my stomach. I fall to the ground, but my teammates jumped Nefaric. It became a full out melee with the Comets and Supernovas brawling for superiority.

"ENOUGH! "said King Saloh from the podium which is centered from the half-field.

"Stop the fighting. Get the Supernovas off the field. The winners of the Allo Cup are the Comets. Nefaric, you ashamed me in from of 700,000 Allonians. You are banned from Allo Ball forever! Get the referee some treatment."

"But father…"

"You disgust me! Get out of my sight!"

Nefaric walks out in humiliation.

"He sounds like a crybaby," I said.

"Nefaric may be a sore loser but he is a competitor. His weakness is his anger. It causes him to do erratic decisions. Once you know his weakness, then you can defeat him. Prepare for the worst. As a reminder, you 33% of ions in Allonian steel but you do not have the other ions from Radium and Gallium. Find them, there's a detector on your wrist. A hologram map will show you where the ions are located. You will need every ounce of energy to defeat Nefaric's Army."

"Yes sir. This will be a challenge."

"Challenges can be conquered. You have the ability to handle this adversity."

I leave the cave and display the map. One ion is in Puerto Rico and the other is in Rio De Janerio? I thought the ions were in North America and Africa? No time to ponder, time to fly.

As I am flying in Brazil, I see the Christ the Redeemer. It's a beautiful statue that watches the city of Rio. The locator brings me to the Corcovado Mountain and locator beeps louder as I land. The ion is beneath the statue and lifted the statue with the gravitational pull method. There it is! It is the Radium ion. The ions automatically retrieve into the medallion and I set the Christ of Redeemer back at its rightful place. Time to travel to Puerto Rico.

The island of Puerto Rico is like heaven. The clear blue ocean tides are enchanting. The ion locator is telling me that the Gallium ion will be in San Juan. Once I landed in San Juan, I had to take advantage of the food. Puerto Ricans are famous for the pernil and I had to take some quality time to eat some of that good pork. There's a nice restaurant called "Amor Rojo" and they served pernil with rice. Mhmm! The food is unbelievably delicious.

After satisfying my stomach, I go focus back to mission. The locator is telling me to go towards Fuerte San Felipe del Morro. The ion energy is beneath the castle near the violent waves below. I hover down, and it is inside a thick brown boulder. With the plasma sword, I carve a hole and the Gallium ion is there. I put the ion in the medallion and fly back home. I do notice with the new ions; my suit is faster and the flight speeds increase dramatically. I can travel from Puerto Rico to Japan less than two minutes.

As I am flying, I am thinking, how the hell did the ions end up in Puerto Rico and Brazil? Also, I notice that the ion energy is not 33%. It's only 15% each which doesn't make any sense when it comes to calculations. There's something odd here and things are not adding up. Did my father transfer all of his knowledge? Shouldn't I know what he knows? Despite the wealth of knowledge, I still have my questions and concerns. Hmm...

CHAPTER 8

NEFARIC'S RETURN

Two weeks passes by and no sign of Nefaric. Did he mean two weeks in Allonian time? If so, it will be a long wait. It's almost summertime and I am graduating from Jen High School with honors. My mother and grandfather are proud of me as I walk down the aisle to accept my diploma. I shake Principal Wong's hand and he whispers in my ear. "You are the late bloomer that shined the brightest. Good luck".

After the ceremony, Tam Hideki comes over to shake my hand.

"Hey, I know I gave you hell for years but I want to say that you're a tough kid. If you need help with anything, here's my business card. The whole Jen High class are celebrating the graduation at my father's famous sushi restaurant. Stop by with your family, it's on me." Tam said.

"Thanks, Tam. We will take that offer." I said.

My family and I enter Tam's sushi restaurant and it is fancy as it comes. The front of the restaurant is a red carpet. There are two butlers that opens your door for you. The floors are marble, and the décor gives you an uppity feeling. Art pieces from the classical periods were hung everywhere. Fish tanks are displaying rare saltwater fish and corrals. The signature Hideki statues and water foundations are present all over the restaurant.

"This is great place, Kenji. Tam is a swell young man to invite us. "said Mom.

"Tam seems like a good kid. Why did you punch him again, Kenji?" said Grandpa.

"Long story. He wasn't this gracious before but let's enjoy the night."
I said.

We sit down at the table and begin to browse through the menu. There
were over a hundred sushi combinations that seem unbelievably delicious.
My grandpa couldn't contain him and salivates on each choice.

"So much sushi and sake! I can't wait to eat and drink it all! "said
Grandpa.

As I glance and observe the room, I see Amaya. She is alone wearing
a beautiful pink dress with her black purse. I wave at Amaya to get her
attention.

"Hey, Amaya come over."

"Ok, Kenji."

Amaya seem very dejected and defeated.

"What's wrong, Amaya? I couldn't find you during the graduation. Is
everything ok?"

"My father never showed up. He is always away for business. I have
no family here."

"I am sorry to hear that. Come join our family. We will make you feel
welcomed."

"Ok, will do."

Amaya joins our table and we are eating unlimited sushi, rice, and
noodles. The night is full of laughter and good conversations. Of course,
my Grandpa needs to embarrass me in front of my girlfriend.

"How does a beautiful young lady like yourself end up with an ugly
kid like Kenji?" said Grandpa.

"Father!" said Mom.

"He's handsome to me. I love Kenji Jackson. He's a sweet young man
with a tender heart."

I get somewhat embarrassed and turn red like a ripe tomato.

"Aww! That is so precious. I am happy that Kenji found a good girl
in Amaya." said Mom.

"I am happy for Kenji too. I can't believe he could find a pretty young
lady when he scares people with his face." Grandpa laughs.

"Come on, Grandpa." I said.

"I am only joking. I need more Sake." Grandpa said.

"I think you need to lay off the Sake." said Mom.

We all laugh and cherish the night. Tam walks in the middle of the restaurant and taps a glass filled with sparkling cider.

"I want to give a toast to our class. We made it. "Tam said. "We did something that was never done before at Jen High. Our class owns the highest-grade point average in school's history. Thanks to one young man that arose to occasion. I must admit that we as student body did not treat this special human being in the correct fashion. This young man has been through thick and thin at Jen High and he managed to have the highest grades in our school's history, even surpassing me. I want to give the honor to the man of the hour that truly deserves recognition and our respect, Kenji Jackson."

The whole restaurant gives me an overwhelming standing ovation with thunderclaps and whistles. Promptly, I become easily mortified. Tam starts waving me to come to his table.

"Make a speech, Kenji. This is your moment." said Tam.

"What?" I said.

"Come up here, Kenji. Make a speech for your class. You deserve this special moment. Don't be shy, kid."

Before I begin to talk, I stare at Amaya and I read her lips. She is saying "you can do it, Kenji". I also see my proud mother in awe. Then, there is Grandpa chugging another bottle of Sake. Tam nudges me.

"Come on Kenji, you got this" Tam encourages.

"Okay, where can I begin. Alright, I want to say thank you Tam Hideki for hosting a fantastic dinner for the class. I don't have a speech prepared so I will wing it. I came a long way. I come from an American Air Force base and didn't know the language of Japanese. I will be frank; I didn't like Jen High. Matter of fact, I despised Jen High from what it represents and their snobby atmosphere which is a facade of reality. I resented the rich spoiled kids that thought they were better due to their lucky circumstances. The wealth that you inherited was not hard work but luck. I didn't have that type of luck. I created it that luck through perseverance and dedication. My vision of becoming something bigger than myself never left my heart and soul. After witnessing my father's death from a plane accident, I promise myself that I honor his death by becoming a decent human being and deliver help to those who need it. I may not have the riches, prestige, or privileges like most of you, but I do feel fortunate to endure the experiences of pain and suffering. Nothing defines character like pain and suffering. It taught me self-reliance, resilience, and tenacity. I inherited those attributes from my grandpa who's the most tenacious man in Japan. I inherited those attributes from mother who works two jobs, so I can go to Jen High. These are adversities that every student in this room are fortunate to never experience but I have been fortunate to endure. My name isn't Hafu. It's Kenji Jackson. I am solid like Steel and will not falter or fail."

At first, there is an awkward silence. Regrettably, I thought I pissed off the whole restaurant with my emotional charged speech. But as I look around, there were tears in the room.

"We are sorry Kenji!" a classmate shout.

"We love you, Kenji." another classmate roars.

The whole room stands up and deliver me another standing ovation. I didn't expect this type of reaction. Some of my classmates came over and embrace me hugs. Tam Hideki walks over and gives me a handshake.

"That was one hell of speech. Very moving. Enjoy the moment."

"Thank you, Tam. I appreciate the kind compliment."

After dinner, my family and Amaya decide to go home. Amaya gives all of us a lift home in her extravagant limousine.

"This is nice. Is there Sake in here?" said Grandpa.

"Grandpa!" I said.

"Mrs. Jackson, is there any way I can stay with your family for the night? I am living alone right now, and my parents are away on business. Sorry for asking or seem like I am imposing." said Amaya.

"No, you're not imposing. It's okay with me. Yes, you can stay at our place. You are always welcomed in the Jackson house. We have a couch that turns into a bed in the living room." said Mom.

"A couch that turns into a bed? That sounds cool! Thank you very much! "said Amaya.

Totally stun by my mother to allow my girlfriend to stay with us. I am kind of flabbergasted that Amaya have the audacity to ask my mother to spend a night at our house. At the same time, I am not in shock either due to my mother's nurturing personality that she is accepting of the favor. The limousine pulls in our driveway and we exit.

"Hey, Phillip pick me up in the morning, "said Amaya.

"Yes, ma'am," said Chauffeur Phillip.

"Good night Phillip! Thank you for the ride and service!" said Mom.

"Hey, Phil! Next time, load up the limousine with some Sake! "said Grandpa.

"Ugh, Grandpa." I said embarrassingly.

My mother makes tea for everybody and we play board games until the late midnight. Grandpa loves to cheat by hiding the game board pieces.

"Grandpa, you will be banned if you don't play by the rules!"

"You just stink at this game Kenji. Stop being a cry-baby!"

"Boys, boys, settle down. It's getting late. Let's all go to bed. Amaya, I have a pajamas and bedsheets with covers in the living room. Time for to hit the sack." said Mom.

"Ok, Mom. I am tired of winning anyways. Grandpa can't beat me without using lame tricks." I said.

"Kenji is upset due to the fact I am superior. Respect your elders." said Grandpa.

"Whatever, dude." I scoff.

"Good night, Amaya," said Mom.

"Good night, Mrs. Jackson. Thank you once again for allowing me to spend the night."

"No problem. I'll make breakfast in the morning."

"Good night, Amaya. See you in the morning, "I said.

"Good night, Kenji." Amaya said in a tender tone.

I switch into my pajamas and jump into bed. Like a bear, I go into hibernation mode in a deep sleep. Dreams begin to happen, and it feels like reality. I am wearing the warrior suit flying towards a volcano. On top of the volcano is Nefaric and he discharges a large energy beam towards me. I couldn't dodge it and become impaired with an injury. I start screaming in pain and crash into the ocean. I wake up in sweat and panting.

"Kenji, are you okay?" said Amaya.

"Yeah, I am okay. I just had a nightmare. Hey, you can't be here."

"I know, I was trying to find the bathroom."

"It's near the kitchen and next to the closet."

"I know, I just wanted to be with you."

"Amaya, you can't be here. What if my mom finds out....

"Shhhh...."

"Amaya, you can't…"

Amaya starts kissing me heavily. My body starts to tingle. One thing led to another and…. I let you imagine what happens next. Not saying a word….

The next morning, I am smiling and fulfill with bliss. I roll over and Amaya is not there. Did she go home? Bacon is in the air and my stomach begins to growl. Breakfast is smelling lovely and I run downstairs for the food. Amaya is chatting with my mother at the kitchen counter.

"How was the bed in the living room? "said Mom.

"It's wonderfully comfortable." said Amaya with a grin. "Better than my bed at home. By the way, the breakfast is scrumptious!"

"Why, thank you! I wish I could get more compliments like this on a daily basis." Mom said.

I can't believe Amaya is lying in front of my mother but I understand. There's a beep outside and it's Phillip.

"Well, thanks for the wonderful breakfast. I must go. My father will be returning for business in the afternoon. Once again, thank you for your generosity."

"No, problem Amaya. Have a lovely day!"

"Give me a kiss goodbye."

Amaya kisses me on the cheek and whispers in my ear.

"Last night was incredible. I love you."

"I love you too."

Amaya exits the door and I watch her leave through the window. The limousine departs and drifts into the sunlight.

"Amaya is a good girl. She is a keeper," said Mom.

"She's wonderful," I said.

"It reminds me when I met your father. He was charming and knew how to make me laugh. That's the key to a relationship. Laughter brings closeness and intimacy. My advice for you two."

"I will remember that Mom. By the way, here's the money I made for the restaurant."

"Thank you, Kenji. Your contributions allow me to work only one job. I appreciate it son."

I gave my mom 600,000 yen which I find it odd that she doesn't questions how I am getting this much money. Maybe, she's content that I am helping with the bills and doesn't ask where it comes from. My mother is an optimistic soul that always has good faith in people including her son. Eventually, I will make my mother the manager of Silver Dreams. Once I solve this potential battle with Nefaric, I will reveal my identity to her. Timing is not right yet.

The television is blaring with breaking news and I see Tokyo in disarray. Debris are in the streets and law enforcement are investigating the vicinity. The news reporter begins to tell the story:

"Two weeks ago, Tokyo was under attack by terrorists that randomly killed 500 people. These heinous criminals used cutting edge technology that is beyond human capabilities. Possibly, these could be aliens from a different planet. As far fetch as that may appears, Japan officials have not found the connection towards the attacks. No country in the world are associated with these unknown terrorists which makes this unfortunate event very peculiar. However, there is pictures and videos of one of terrorist in Brazil and Puerto Rico. Here is video from Rio de Janerio."

"Dear lord!" said Mom. "He is lifting the Christ Redeemer!"

"Oh boy…" I said under my breath.

Here are more photos of the terrorist in San Juan, Puerto Rico. Are our days on Earth numbered? NATO forces are joining the fight for Japan as this is a world issue and concern.

"We will support the Japan in this fight. The United States of America represents democracies around the world. We do not support terrorism and will protect our allies and special interests. Japan, we have your back!" said the President of United States.

"Terrorism is not tolerated. We shall support Japan if attacks arrive, "said President of France.

"One team, one fight. We will be there when time arrives again." said United Kingdom Prime Minister.

"This is getting scary, Kenji." said Mom.

"Yes, this is concerning." I said.

"One thing that's good coming out of tragedy is other countries are putting their differences aside and working together as a team." said Grandpa.

"That's one way to put it. I just wonder if they will attack again." said Mom.

That question has not been answered. No sign of Nefaric and it's getting worrisome.

Four weeks later, nothing changes. Is Nefaric bluffing? What is his strategy? I continue my life but always have that pondering thought of Nefaric's return in the back of my head. The Summer Olympics are in Tokyo and the city is ecstatic to host the great games. The opening ceremony is tonight, and Amaya got tickets to the event. Her father is a sponsor for the Olympics and have purchase close seats to the event. Security is on high alert and there were soldiers all over the city and outside the stadium. Amaya and I sit in the front row to watch the show and the atmosphere electrifying. Fireworks are bursting which paints the skies like a mural. The athletes all over the world are marching with pride representing their countries. A litany of presidents and leaders were present waving to the crowds One of the survivors of Nefaric's attacks lit the torch and the whole crowd roars in honor.

The night is almost flawless until an ominous cloud hovers the stadium. An eerie red-light pierce through the cloud. Immediately, I know it is Nefaric! The athletes run inside the stadium and the crowd screams in fright. Some attendees are frozen in fear and others are running for safety. A spaceship appears and lands in the middle of the stadium. Doors open from the spaceship and it's Nefaric slowly walking down with his soldiers. It's time to act.

"I gotta go. Amaya, leave the stadium now!"

"What do you mean, is this part of the show?"

"Amaya, just do what I say. Get out of here now! I will call you later but there's something I must do."

"Alright. I don't understand but okay."

I run throughout the stadium to find a go place to change into the Warrior-suit. Hysteria is spreading amongst the crowd as spectators are attempting to exit. I see a janitor's closet and open the door to get into battle mode. I transform into the Warrior-suit and fly back inside. Nefaric takes a microphone from the Olympics announcer and starts speaking.

"Where is Kenji? Come now to center stage!"

"Right here!" I said as I hover down onto the stadium grounds.

"Sorry that I was tardy. Wars have no timeline and had businesses to take care of. Are you ready to be King of Alloy?"

"Yes, I am. I am ready to be King of Alloy. It's an absolute honor to lead the Allonian people to glory and prosperity. However, I will not give up the medallion. There's too much good that the AFOP can bring to the people of Alloy, Radium, and Gallium. AFOP can rebuild all three planets and generate power to restore the damages and destruction from war. There's no need for me to forfeit the medallion as I see it as a tool for advancement rather than a detriment to the gods. After meticulously researching the options for the medallion, I think the best decision is to keep device and reconcile all three planets with an eternal peace treaty. As gods, there's no reason or justification to continue a war base on an unfortunate misunderstanding."

"An unfortunate misunderstanding? Tell those asinine words to the families of Alloy that perished over the AFOP. Tell the Alloy soldiers who sacrificed their lives over the AFOP. An offensive statement by a foolish extension of Candor! You won't hand over the medallion? Fine, I declare war upon Earth. We will obliterate every person and creature on this planet and claim it ours. Traitors to our race will not be tolerated. Time for this planet to burn and die!"

Nefaric raises his arm directly to the audience and blast a fireball which creates an explosion! Half the stadium dwindles into pieces.

"Consider this action as a warning shot. Allonians take pride in warfare. Get your troops ready, I will meet you in Tokyo no later than noon. I want a fair fight so when I defeat you, ultimate humiliation shall rise upon you. Then, you will burn in hell."

Nefaric takes the microphone one last time and stares at the media cameras to broadcast his wicked message in front of the whole world.

"Hello, Earth. I am Nefaric. I am the King of Alloy. I will reign genocide to this putrid planet and prepare for your death. I shall return the next sunrise and exterminate each of you one by one. This planet was a haven for a criminal and pariah to our planet Alloy. His name is being Candor, my brother and traitor to our beloved Alloy. You kept him safe and protected him for years! Tomorrow will be the day of retribution. Bring all your military to the battlefield. You do not stand a chance against a God! Save your impractical prayers for mercy, there will be none. Precipitation of death shall fall upon you."

Nefaric leaves in his spaceship with his soldiers. The NATO forces from all nations arrive late to the stadium come to arrest me! At least 50,000 soldiers with tanks and rifles were pointing their weapons towards me. Apache helicopters were hovering the stadium and my ears feels like I am inside a hornet's nest.

"Point your hands up! Do not move or we will shoot you! Get on your knees with your hands in the air!" said U.S. General Coakley through a megaphone.

Knees plants on the ground and the troops arrest me. The NATO Forces transport me to the Okinawa, my first home.

CHAPTER 9

WAR OF THE STEEL ROSES

NATO Forces put me in a prison chamber which is effortlessly escapable. The warden transports me in handcuffs towards the interrogation room. Inside the interrogation room were high ranking military officials and president of the United States and Japan Prime Minister. General Coakley starts shouting at me.

"Look at me in the eyes. Why are you here on Earth? Tell me you scumbag. Take off your helmet." scolds General Coakley.

"No, I will not take it off. It's gratuitous and not necessary."

"Take your helmet off! It's a direct order from the General and the president of the United States." General Coakley said with a hoarse tone.

"No dishonor to the president but I am not taking off the helmet. It's part of my uniform."

"You piece of shit!" curses General Coakley.

General Coakley slaps me, but I am not phased. It feels like a soft pillow brushing my face.

"No need for violence. I can easily breakout of these handcuffs and put you in your place. You're probably uninformed and ignorant, but I am American like you. I was born here in Japan on this exact U.S. Air Force base. My name is Kenji Jackson, son of Conway Jackson."

"Conway Jackson? The Major Conway Jackson? The great pilot?" said General Coakley.

"Yes, I am Kenji Jackson. I am just as American as you are sir! Four

Scores and seven years ago…I am not your enemy. Nefaric is the enemy that you want to extinguish, not me."

I stand up and the soldiers begin to panic. Guns are drawn. Clicking of multiple bolts sounds like a firework show. They were pointing their weapons, but I sense their fear. I had to calm the soldiers down and reassure that I am their ally.

"Don't move an inch or we will shoot!"

"I can easily eliminate each one of you with one attack. I came in peace."

I break the handcuffs and it drops to the ground.

"See, I am not a threat. Drop your weapons."

"General Coakley, tell your men to drop their weapons. I think we have an ally on our side." said the President of the United States.

"Gentlemen, disengage!"

The soldiers drop their rifles in perfect unison.

"Listen, president. Your weapons are no match for these guys. These are gods."

"Gods? The only god I know is in the good ole' Bible. King version to be exact." said General Coakley.

"Believe, what you want to believe, but these beings are superior to human. They possess technology lightyears ahead from Earth's technology. The Allonians can destroy this planet within seconds. The only thing that's giving us time is their formality to war. Allonians like to fight one on one at certain time and date. It's our saving grace and we need to strategize."

"What should we do, Kenji?", said the President of the United States.

"With all due respect, Mr. President. Why should we trust this whatever he is?" said General Coakley.

"I think we have no choice but to trust him," said Japan Prime Minister "My people have suffered enough, and I am desperate to end these attacks. Kenji comes across as a friend more than a foe."

"I agree with the Prime Minister. Kenji has insight and intel that we do not have now. Neither the FBI nor CIA can trace these adversaries. Kenji, the world needs your service. What should we do? "said the President of the United States.

"Give me all of your weapons and artillery. I will modify your weapons to counter the Allonian soldiers. M-16 rifles, tanks, ballistic missiles, or anything you have on hand, give it to me. Engineering is in my background. My late father is an expert in manufacturing and assemble devices which he taught he well. With my assistance, I will lead the NATO Forces to victory."

"Leading the brave men and women to battle is my job," said General Coakley.

"I am the commander in chief. I will make the decisions here. General Coakley, you will assist Kenji. This is our best weapon we have against this type of war. This isn't conventional warfare. We must listen to Kenji and he knows the enemy better than us. I have no choice. This Nefaric character will come destroy again. I will do what you say Kenji."

"I will not let you down President and Prime Minister." I said.

"General Coakley, please lead Kenji to the artillery." said President of the United States.

"Sir, yes, sir," General Coakley said with a firm salute.

General Coakley leads to all the artillery and aircrafts. Every weapon I touch, I created a mini plasma blaster that can eliminate an Allonian. Modified over 500,000 M16 less than an hour. I implement new weaponry for the tanks and aircrafts which can combat with Allonian strength. The weapons have a set time limit for only this battle. No AFOP mistake will happen on Earth.

"All weapons are modified and ready for war," I said.

"That was swift. Can we see a test?" said General Coakley.

"Yes, you can. Give me a target."

"We will use a broken vehicle," said General Coakley. "I will take you to a secure area to demonstrate your modifications."

General Coakley takes me to an open field and one of the soldiers have a modified M-16. All NATO personnel are watching the demonstration.

"Hello, ladies and gentlemen. This is my demonstration of the modified M-16. You can't defeat an Allonian with conventional military weapons because it will not be effective. The weaponry on Earth is too slow and will not cause any significant damage towards the Allonian Army. However, with my expertise, I will show how we can defeat them. Watch as this soldier shoots at this vehicle with a standard M-16 rifle."

The U.S. Army private shoots at the vehicle.

"Bare minimum damage. Now shoot with the modified M-16"

As the Army Private begins to aim, his rifle begins to glow blue and the NATO personnel start gasping in amazement. The Army Private shoots and a plasma ray blasts through the muzzle. The car blows out into millions of fragments.

"This is the type of artillery that you will need against the Allonian Army. I enhanced every vehicle, aircraft, and weapon as much as possible. Do you have any questions?"

The NATO personnel had nothing to say except the Prime Minister of Japan.

"We are blessed to have Kenji on our side. We will win this war!"

NATO cheers with enthusiasm and though I galvanize the NATO forces, I am terrified inside. Will I succeed? Will I be able to defeat Nefaric and his robust army? Do I have enough training from my father? I am worried because I am inexperienced. I do not know what to expect. These Allonians are battle tested and fought in many wars against Gods, not people. Allonians are powerful beings that can destroy the humans less than a second. I am worried that I will fail but I must not lose faith.

"Prime Minister, I think you should tell your citizens in Tokyo to evacuate the city."

"I am right ahead of you, Kenji. We have thousands of busses for transportations as we speak. We do not want or can afford any more casualties. I want my people to safe from this war. I fear for the worst."

"Don't worry Prime Minister, I will not let the country of Japan and the rest of the world down. Am I free to go?"

"Yes, please meet the NATO forces at 09:00."

"Yes, sir."

Before leaving the Air Force base, I had to go back where tragedy began in my life. With permission, I am able to walk on the flight line where my father died from Nefaric's cowardly attack. It's funny and ironic how life goes in full circle and I am back where life changed for me. The feeling is surreal and captivating. Old feelings and sentiments engulf my soul and I begin to cry. It's like I am traveling to memory lane with hundreds of reminiscences flowing through my mind. The air shows seeing the Blue Angels in the air, playing football during recess, and hearing the airmen march and "Reveille" in the mornings. These are memories that I will cherish with every vessel in my heart.

I deeply miss my father being alive and not just a spirit that's limited to a mountain. Times were precious back then and carefree. That sense of peace in mind no longer exists since that day. Watching my father in a casket dropping six feet under will forever etched in my memory. This is why I can never forgive what Nefaric did to my father. Though he made swaying points about protecting the Alloy, however, there's no justification for the slaying my father. Verbal exchanges could have been conducted but he decided to kill without remorse or warning. A spineless chemo-lightning shot to kill my father? A so-called warrior and Chief of Forces can only defeat someone from a distance? That's not honor! That's a disgrace! It's time to take my place as the King of Alloy! It's time to fulfill my destiny and bring the equilibrium back to the three planets. Time to end the reign of Nefaric! This is for my father Candor. The time is 21:59 with sixty seconds left until they play Taps. I fly over my father's grave as the melancholy song plays throughout the base. I give my father a salute for his service and always being there for me, even beyond death.

Urgently, I fly back home and change back to my street clothes. I walk inside the living room and there's my mother and grandpa staring at me with rage.

"Where were you? I am worried sick!" cries Mom. "I thought something bad happened. It's 11:59!"

"You forgot to feed the chickens, harvest the rice, and clean the dojo," yells Grandpa. "You also missed our Samurai training!"

With the war among us, I must reveal to my Mom and Grandpa the god-honest truth about my identity, my father, and possibly my final mission to save Earth.

"I am deeply sorry Mom and Grandpa. I am truly am. Ok, this will be very awkward and uncomfortable, but I have to tell you the truth."

"Truth? Did you get Amaya pregnant? I don't mind having a grand-baby." said Mom.

"No! No, no, no, it's not that."

"Did Amaya breakup with you?" questions Grandpa. "I guess she bought new glasses and saw that hideous face of yours. I would runaway myself if I weren't so old."

"You have jokes, Grandpa. But seriously, I have to tell both of you the truth and sit down when I say it."

Grandpa and Mom sit down on the couch while drinking some tea.

"Ok.....what is it son?" Mom said.

"I am a god from a different planet."

"What? Ha, ha, ha, ha!" laughs Mom "I gave birth to you. There's no way. I am not the virgin Mary."

"Are you joking Kenji? This is hilarious." Grandpa said with a belly of laughter "If you're a god, how come you didn't do your chores on time?"

"Oh my god, Grandpa! No pun intended. Alright, I will show you since you don't believe the words coming out of my mouth." I said with frustration and determination to enlighten these two goofballs.

I transform into the Warrior-suit and both stopped laughing.

"See, I am a God from planet Alloy."

"Nice Halloween costume," said Grandpa. "I am impressed but I still don't believe you're a God."

(Sigh) "Ok, I will have to show you more."

I begin to utilize gravitational powers and lifted the pot of tea. I pour a cup for my Grandpa.

"Nice magic trick, Kenji. You should do shows in Las Vegas." said Grandpa.

"My lord, you are hard to persuade! Forget it. I will show you and Mom at Mount Tenchi."

"Kenji, Mount Tenchi is three hours away." said Mom.

"Not with my flight speed. Come outside with me."

"Flight speed? Is that a new drug?" said Grandpa.

Grandpa and Mom followed me towards the outside and I have two spherical pods that I developed for flight passengers laying in the backyard. They are made from silver steel with comfortable seating, radio, and thick glass window for view. During flights, I will utilize gravitational heave to levitate the pods as I travel through the skies.

"These are my steel pods for flight. Hop right in." I said.

"Flight? Is this another magic trick?" said Grandpa.

"Grandpa, you're being annoying. Just get in already. You too, Mom."

"Don't sass me young boy!" said Grandpa.

(Sigh) "Just do it." I said.

"Kenji, what are we doing?" Mom said with great concern. 'I don't understand what is going on. Can we get these silver balls off my lawn?

They are eyesores and ruining the curb appeal. I am planning to garden there and it's in the way!"

"Guys, relax! Just humor me. Jump inside the pod."

"Ok, Mr. God. Ha-ha! What a goof," said Grandpa.

"Ok, honey but make it quick. I have to go to bed for my beauty sleep," said Mom.

(eyeroll) "Party poopers…."

Mom and Grandpa sit inside the pod and lock the hatchet. I turn on my jets and activate the gravitational heave.

"We are floating!" said Mom with excitement.

"Ok, nice magic trick. Can we leave now?" Grandpa said in full sarcasm.

"It's only the beginning. Put on your seatbelts. This will be the most exciting ride in your life. On three, two, one, and………………….. LAUNCH!"

As I blast into the air, I hear my Mom and Grandpa screaming. One is screaming with fear and other with joy.

"Awwwwwwwwwwwwwww! Kenji, you're going to be grounded when you get home! But first put this pod on the ground!" yells Mom.

"Wooooooooooooooo! This is cool!" yells Grandpa with glee.

We land on Mount Tenchi and navigate them inside the cave where my father dwells.

"I hope by now you believe that I am God from Alloy. If not, this will convince you. Father, I need you to appear."

"Kenji? Are you delusional? We are in the middle of a cave with bats flying around. Why are you calling for your father? He's no longer with us."

"No, I am with you now" said Candor.

"Oh, my heavens!" said Grandpa.

"Conway? Is this really you? I missed you so much. Why are you here? How is this possible? I saw you die on the flight line and watch the casket drop down to the ground. Were you here the whole time? I need you back in my life!" said Mom while crying.

Candor wipes the mother's tears and gives her a long and warm hug.

"Yes, this is me. I miss you too my love. But I must say, I am not Conway. My name is Candor from another planet called Alloy. There's a litany of things I must tell you and your father. Please bear with me."

Candor explains in full detail about his origins to Mom and Grandpa and they are finally convinced that we were Gods. My mother becomes a sphere of emotions with resentment, confusion, clarity, happiness, sadness, and acceptance. Mom didn't appreciate that Candor was keeping a surplus of secrets from her, but she understood the justification.

"I wish you told me on day one," said Mom. "I would've accepted for who you are. There's no need to hide secrets from your wife. We should be able to tell each other anything. I love Conway, I mean Candor."

"Babe, you can call me Conway." said Father. "I like Conway more, sounds sexier."

Both of my parents share a laugh as I roll my eyes in disgust and embarrassment.

"Can you come home with us?" said Mom.

"No, I must remain here. My spirit is alive, but I can't return to the living world with full autonomy. Perhaps, Kenji can find a way to revive my life back but at this moment, I have to stay here."

"I will visit you every day. I must be with my husband." said Mom. "If I must move near Mount Tenchi, it's something I shall do."

"You don't have to sacrifice for me. Find a new husband that will provide the love and care that I cannot provide at this time. I won't be jealous or envious. Timokko, I want to see you happy."

"You are my happiness. It's ok, I rather have you here and not have you at all."

"Ok, dear if you insist. I will always be here. I have no choice."

"My son-in-law is royalty? Unbelievable! I just want to apologize by the way I treated you over the years. We took care of Kenji and he grew up to be a true gentleman. His characteristics come from you. I just want to say thank you."

"I appreciate it. Mr. Lin." said Candor.

"You can call me Dad. "said Grandpa

"Ok......Dad." replied Candor with puzzlement.

"I don't mean to rush but I have to leave now. There is a war among us, and I have to report in Tokyo as soon as possible." I said.

"War? What do you mean Kenji?" said Mom.

"Tomorrow, Nefaric will attack Tokyo. Currently, I am the leader of the NATO Forces and I will conduct warfare against the Allonian

Army. The Prime Minister of Japan is counting on me. The whole world is putting their faith upon my shoulders. This is my purpose in life, serve and protect the planet Earth."

"Son, I don't want you to fight. I lost my husband and I do not want to lose my only son. I can't bear another day if I lose you, Kenji!"

"I promise I will return to you, Mom. I have to save the world from Nefaric's destruction. Father can elaborate more about the quagmire, but I have to go. I think it's best if you and Grandpa stay here. It's safe. Inside the pods, I stored an abundance of food and water. The pod also transforms into a bed, so you can rest. You will be okay inside of Mount Tenchi."

"Ok, Kenji. Please return safe and sound. I love you, son."

My mother kisses me on forehead and gave me a tight hug. I see Grandpa in a corner of the cave, and I heard some sniffling. Is he crying?

"Grandpa, are you alright?"

"Yes, yes. I worry about you Kenji. You grew so fast and I do not want you to leave Earth under these circumstances. I do not want to see my grandson in a casket. You should bury me. I just hope my Samurai training will be accommodating to the battlefield."

"Grandpa, no need to lose faith. I am a Samurai like you! I will survive."

"Make me proud, Kenji."

Grandpa gives me a bow. I return the favor with a bow as well. It's the ultimate honor coming from him.

"Kenji, you are an Allonian. Allonians never falter. I provided you the knowledge and training. Believe in your teachings. You are the King of Alloy, return Alloy to glory!"

"Yes, father!"

Father stands in attention and give me a salute. I salute back with pride. The wings spread, and I soar out of the cave towards Tokyo.

The sun is bright, and the air is crisp. My mind and emotions are flowing heavily and it's difficult to concentrate. Will I be able to complete the mission? Anxiety is manifesting and doubts somewhat tiptoes in my mind. I can't be scared. If I perish, it's with honor. Death will not defeat me.

As I glide through the air, I see the skyline of Tokyo. It's a ghost town, no citizens are roaming around the city. It's an unnerving feeling to see a city that's thriving suddenly dies with activity. No sight of Nefaric which is his modus operandi. Giving direct times isn't Nefaric's strength but his tardiness could present as a military strategy. The only population is the NATO Forces with tanks, helicopters, and 500,000 soldiers and personnel in downtown Tokyo. General Coakley is directing the troops and conveying a full briefing for the mission.

"Alright, you brave men and women. This fight is not just for the support relief to Japan but the entire world. This is the first time in world history that all countries come together as cohesive unit. We have Non-NATO members willing to sacrifice their lives. That's a true testimony of humanity. Despite our different beliefs, governments, and backgrounds, we are all hear to reach our common goal which is eliminating these foreigners from a different planet. This is our Earth, our land. We shall defend it!"

All 500,000 soldiers roar in unison.

"We must cover every inch of the city and exterminate anything that's moving. Also…Kenji you're late!"

"Sorry, sir. I had to take care of my family."

"It's your time to take care of the world. Ladies and gentlemen, this is your leader Kenji. He's a special person with capabilities that we don't have. Listen to him. Son, do you have a plan?"

"Yes, I will take care of Nefaric, the leader of the Allonian Army. Just take care of the fleet of Allonian soldiers that are coming in full force. They have enhanced aircrafts, tanks, and weapons that are superior to human technology. However, do not get discouraged, soldiers. Do not panic, and do not lose faith with each other. With the new installments that I implemented in your artillery, you can and will defeat these barbarians. Take pride and honor for Earth. We shall eradicate them for trespassing our lands. Don't be afraid, don't let fear dictate your actions. Put the fear in them. You have full control of your purpose and destiny. I am honored to fight along with the best of best men and women in the Armed Forces. Let's prepare for battle!"

"Hear that! Let's take care of business. Let's take back, Earth!"

The soldiers roar louder than before but immediately becomes silence. Up in the skies are hundreds of spacecrafts appearing. Some land on the skyscrapers, others on the streets. Simultaneously, the spacecrafts open their doors and thousands of solders run full speed with their weapons.

Watching the battle-ready Allonian soldiers gave me severe anxiety. The Allonian Army were crawling everywhere in masses and overconsuming the city. Usually, I put up a good poker face, but I am trembling in my knees. Am I ready for this? General Coakley startles me with his yelling of commands.

"Time to engage!" said General Coakley.

Then, reality finally hits me. I transform from graduating high school to a soldier. How did I get here? The outline of my future is not this moment but I must own it. There is no choice, this is destiny. Sometimes in life you are put in uncomfortable circumstances, but you know your true character when you overcome adversity. This war will be named "War of the Steel Roses". Hearts of compassion become colder than steel which contains prickly thorns of pain and anguish. The entire complexity of the war is based on a misunderstanding. Both sides possess strong convictions on who is right. People will die, Allonians will die. I never killed anyone except a few insects in my life. It's not in my nature but there's a period in life where you are required to be out of character to survive. This will be the time.

CHAPTER 10

DERKINS' DECEPTION

The Allonian Army is marching in full speed towards the NATO Forces. Suddenly, the Allonian Army goes in formation in columns and lifting their knees high.

"Hold your fire." said General Coakley.

"Eee Napa Dorac Goluki Gah! ('Infantry Post Front and Center' in Allonian)" said Nefaric.

Nefaric suddenly appears in the front of his Army and begins to speak.

"Ah, at last we meet again. "said Nefaric as he stares directly in my eyes.

"We will end this score today. Our soldiers are prepared for battle. We can end this battle if you surrender." said General Coakley.

"Ha-ha-ha! Confidence I see, but very delusional indeed. Step aside peasant, I want to speak to the true leader here on Earth. You don't seem to have the proper prestige to carry a conversation with an Allonian."

"Hey, no need to be discourteous." I said. "I don't understand why you have the desire for devastation and destruction. There's no need to harm or kill the people on Earth. This isn't their fight. There's no need to have your men and women in harm's way for a superficial reason. The AFOP can help Alloy, Radium and Gallium return to healthy status. My father's goal was to unite the Gods and exist in peace. I do not want to fight, Nefaric but I will defend my planet if necessary. This will be your final opportunity to disengage in war and return to Alloy with no repercussions.

It will be advantageous for both parties and I am willing to go to Alloy to repair the damages of war. Do you accept my offering?"

"Absolutely.......... not! How dare you call yourself an Allonian? You worse than your pathetic father! Putting these weak earthlings before a God? Your pacifistic ideals and concepts show how feeble you are as God. The hereditarily human trait is your ultimate flaw. Compassion and empathy will be your definitive downfall. You are still trusting your father's litany of lies as facts. A son's bias to their father's words are bound to always happen. However, your father is not present to save you. With your decision of not forfeiting the medallion, you're principally exposing that all the Allonian lives that perished under the AFOP Act died in vain. Many Allonians suffered from your father's detrimental invention for energy. Alloy was thriving and doing quite well before he introduced the divisive AFOP ACT. Now the planet is in ruins and imbalanced with continual chaos. Fine, you decided your fate. I will seal it. I have given you ample time to adjust your mind but you're more asinine than your father. You're not worthy or a true Allonian God! I will let my soldiers kill you before you have an opportunity to face me! I will let my elite commanders handle the mission. This isn't worth my duration. Allonians.......... ATTACK!"

Nefaric disappears and war begins in a flash. The Allonians begin to march towards the troops.

"NATO Forces take out the ground troops. I will take care of the flying aircrafts."

Allonians draws plasma swords and cannons. NATO Forces draw their weapons as well. Allonians attacks first with plethora of lasers, rays, and beams towards the troops. The energy attack is coming at a rapid pace and I decide to use gravitational heave to halt the devastation. I thrust the beam in reverse towards the Allonian Army and became a direct hit towards the Allonian front lines.

"This is your chance! Go attack now! The front line is vulnerable. Take them out! "The NATO Forces become overwhelm with exuberance and counterattacks the Allonian Army. The fight the ground is gruesome and fierce, but the humans have an upper hand with their new upgraded weapons. I take myself to the skies to take out the aircrafts. The plasma sword is displaying in my hand which I split into two for the discs. I rotate the swords and toss the discs towards multiple aircrafts causing all of them to explode. Glove blasters were in full effect to take out more aircrafts and reinforcements. Chaos is brewing, and destruction is present. Buildings were falling like trees and crumbling like leaves. Lives were being lost on both sides, but humans are winning the battle.

"Keep it up, Soldiers! We are halfway there." I said.

As the Allonians were battling the ground troops, I am searching for Nefaric through the air. He tends to go incognito and I begin to call his name out.

"Where are you, coward? Where are you Nefaric? Come fight me like a man!"

A random voice echoes.

"You have to get through me first before you can approach the true King of Alloy."

It is Lt. Major Barium or as known as Captain Derkins. His armor resembles my armor but slightly thinner with metallic green and mauve colors. Barium drapes a long cape that is stitched with Allonian lettering and symbols. The ultimate con man and actor that can make Hollywood envious. To disguise yourself as fellow airmen to help an assassination mission is truly sociopathic and downright evil. My father trusted Captain Derkins and loved him like a brother. Captain Derkins is wickedness personified.

"Captain Derkins. You are the one who sold out my father. How could you?"

"The name is Lt. Major Barium. I follow orders from the Chief of Forces and executed the mission. Your father Candor was a good man, but I prioritize my planet before anything else. My core values are to protect and serve the Gods of Alloy. Your father was no longer a God of Alloy. He betrayed his people and left them to die. My assignment was to deliver his demise and it was a pleasure to watch him croak."

"You are a heartless bastard!"

"Heartless? Perhaps. Do I regret my actions? Never! I am the Chief of Espionage. Our core mission is to dissect information for the sole purpose to counter our adversaries. Your father is the enemy. My purpose is to terminate the threat."

"Candor wasn't a threat, but I will become your threat. Today is the impeccable time to end your life! Captain Derkins, Barium, or scumbag,

I will eliminate your existence for my father! Deception does not give you honor!"

Quickly, I draw my sword. The plasma blade is in full strength. Lt. Major Barium draws his sword, but it is crafted in a grotesque way. There are three plasma blades on each side of the long cylinder handle.

"Deception is the key element to war. It's necessary and intelligent. To defeat a neophyte like yourself in war, it takes less than a second. I am not in the shadows; I am in the sunlight ready to obliterate you and this primitive planet."

Barium strikes first and I counter with my sword. Clashing of swords are fierce and going at a rapid pace. Grandpa's teachings from the samurai ways are elevating my swordsmanship. In Barium's eyes, he looks puzzled in confusion.

"You are better than I previously thought. "said Barium.

"My primitive planet taught me how to fight!" I said proudly.

"I like a challenge, but I will not concern." Barium said.

The sword fight becomes extremely close. I swing and miss. Barium swings and he miss. Clashing of the plasma blades causes a chain reaction of energy and heat. Sweat drips in my suit from the heavy labor of battle. Barium seems to be fatigue as well as I give him all of what I got.

"You're good for a novice but take this you bastard!" screams Barium

Barium shoots a beam from his sword and I deflect the beam towards the ocean. Barium's beam creates a large whirlpool and I see a killer whale swirling in the cycle. His attack would have devastated half of Tokyo.

"That was close, but no cigar." I said with a big grin.

Barium grinds his teeth in frustration and lunges with his sword. Swords clash like lightening and made thunderous sounds. As we exchange sword swings in midair, Barium suddenly disappears.

"I have no time to play these hide-and-go seek. Come out and fight!"

Suddenly, there are five Bariums! Clones of him surrounding me and pointing their plasma swords.

"See this is my multi-technique. You think that you can fight all five of me!"

The multiple Barium threw a monkey wrench in my focus. Suddenly, all five Bariums come lunging in a full attack. Plasma swords were swinging in all directions, but I counter of them. Though there were five Bariums, the attacks were significantly weaker and slower. With each counter, I stabbed a Barium in the heart which the illusion disappears in an instant. One by one, Bariums vanishes until there were two.

"Your strategies are weak, Barium. You thought this was a challenge?"

"I have more tricks up my sleeve. Don't get too cocky. You will die upon my hands."

The two Bariums started to charge up their hands with ball of energy and launch beams towards me. I discontinue the beams with gravitational heave and reverse the direction, so he can taste his own medicine. One hit Barium directly and other Barium dodged it.

"There's the real Barium!"

I glide directly to Barium and uppercut him in the jaw. He falls in the ocean and a large splash immerse. As I hover over the splash, I am anticipating his return from the water. A few minutes passes by and no sign of Barium.

"Barium, I know you are alive! Come out the water, you clown!"

More minutes go by and no Barium.

"Come out and fight!" I yell.

"Look up, you simpleton!" Barium laughs.

Barium is hovering above and attempts to strike at my head. In the nick of time, I block his sword. Barium strikes with abundance of force, but I am able to hold him off.

"Nice counter but how about this!" Barium hollers.

A small ball rolls upon Barium's hands and turns into gas. Some reason, I can't breathe, and I am gasping for air. I fall to the ground and crash into a newspaper kiosk. Paper and candy flutters on me. Soda bottles are spilling in the streets and I hear the sizzling popping of the carbonation. There's only darkness and lost vision. I am assuredly blind and can't get any oxygen.

"This is my paralysis smoke. This gas agent will keep you paralyzed for a few moments. Kenji, you're a fool. Deception will always be a strategic tactic with the Allonian Army. It's something that you never learned on this lower tier planet. Kenji, I warned you about me and I shall finish the deed."

It seems like my senses are out of whack. The only thing I could see is dimness and thin spark of light from the sun. I heard Barium's raspy voice, but I couldn't see the bastard. However, I feel the heatwaves from his sword and counter his attack with my plasma blade.

"Huh?" said Barium.

With conviction, I stand up with confidence and determination.

"I can't see but I can still smell a rat!" I said. "Next time, take a bath you dirty weasel!"

I felt his body temperature and smelled his funky stench. With one attack, I deliver a demoralizing and devastating beam to his stomach. The energy beam is very potent in which Barium flies into a skyscraper.

"Ahhhhhhh!" yells Barium.

BOOM! Windows are bursting and shattering towards the ground. Loud noises of crumbling and implosion trembles in my ears. As I crawl onto the ground to find a water bottle from the newspaper stand. Swiftly, I take off my helmet and pour the liquid onto my face. Regrettably, it is orange soda which burn my eyes worse than the paralysis gas! In a panic, I quickly scurry for another bottle and it is fresh, cool, and soothing water. My eyes feel refresh and I can see once again. I finish drinking the bottle of water and continue the search for Barium. Heavy breathing and panting echoes from a half-destroyed building. It is Barium who is barely hanging on a thread as he lays on concrete rubble.

"How did you know to counter my attack? No enemy could recover from my tactics. "said Barium.

"Deception is for the weak. What is kept in the darkness will eventually come to the light. You are too slow with your weaponry. Countering your attacks were easy. My grandfather taught me focus and discipline when it comes to swordsmanship. My father taught me honor and respect. What you did to my father is spineless. Allonians aren't fragile Gods that need to resort to cheap tricks. From Allonian to another Allonian, you have neither integrity nor honor. You are nothing but a complete disgrace!" I said.

"Go fuck yourself!" Barium said to me while spitting purple blood.

"This is for Candor. Go to hell."

With strong conviction, I take my sword and stab him in the heart with a death blow. Barium instantaneously becomes lifeless and I have no remorse for his soul. One chapter is closed, time to take the throne from Nefaric.

CHAPTER 11

ROYAL RETRIBUTION

After defeating Barium, I continue to maintain a calm rage. The fighting spirit implements in my soul, but I am in complete control. The Allonian essence is in my ambiance and the quiet storm is brewing in my mind. Nefaric needs to pay for what he did to my father and the planet Alloy. I am flying in mid-air searching for the master of destruction. It seems like hiding is his favorite strategy which fits his narrative of cowardice.

Skyscraper to skyscraper, I am gliding through the metro and no Nefaric. I become extremely vexed and become enraged with impatience.

"Nefaric, I do not have time for your mindless games. Where the hell are you! Come out and fight me like a man!"

"I am not a man; I am a God!" yells Nefaric from an unknown area.

Suddenly, a random red beam hits my back and I fall straight into a skyscraper window! Glass shatters and concrete walls cracks. No damage to the Warrior-suit but I am slightly bruised. The impact of Nefaric's energy beams are stronger than I thought and made me slightly paralyze momentarily. The blast decibels were so loud that I became deaf in my right ear for few seconds. I get up, wipe the debris from my suit and draw my sword.

"Enough with these sporadic attacks. I am standing here, Nefaric. Let's fight one on one. You want this medallion, come take it!"

Nefaric is nowhere to be found. He kept playing vexing mind games that made me insane. I hear his voice but still cannot find him. It sounds like whispers in my ear but no sign of Nefaric.

"Stop this bullshit! Where are you! Come and get me you punk!"

"Ha-ha-ha! Am I getting under your thin skin?" said Nefaric. "Your mind is feeble and limited. How you are Allonian yet can't detect my energy? You're a novice in combat and it is evident. If you were in my Army, you wouldn't survive in basic training. You are rubbish!"

"Nefaric, shut the hell up! Where are y...!"

BAM! I feel a knuckled-punch out of nowhere and fall from the air to the ground. A city bus breaks my fall and folds an origami. Gingerly, I stand up, but I feel the impact.

"Fuck! That hurts!" I said. "He must be using incognito mode. Two can play that game."

It is my turn for incognito mode to level out the playing field. This time, I can see his body heat and movements. Nefaric is behind me and on top of a bridge discharging two beams. From my father's teachings, I dodge the beam and deflect the other one. However, the two beams ricochets into an arena and obliterates the establishment. Signs of advertisements from the arena broke into a million of pieces. Debris is in the winds covering the streets. Thank goodness no civilians are present, but the destruction is very severe.

"His power is phenomenal. How the hell did he achieve this power?"

Nefaric is extremely agile and swift. His military suit is faster than my Warrior-suit which I find jarring. His armor design is sleek, less bulky, and there's four wings on the back which resemblance a dragonfly. His experience in flight is conspicuous as he lunges with supreme quickness towards me. I take a swing with my plasma sword, but he disappears. I become confuse.

"Huh?"

"Pee-A-Boo!" Nefaric said in a mocking fashion.

Nefaric punches me in the gut and this time, I felt true pain. Blood spits out my mouth.

"I thought this would somewhat challenging but why am I mildly surprised? Your inexperience is obvious. Do you know who I am? I am the Chief of Forces with over a thousand wars, combats, and battles under my belt. Staining the enemy is my calling and duty. With your novice level of combat, it's obviously clear that you will never be King!"

Nefaric clenches his hands together and raises them high.

"This is for Alloy, you descendant of a traitor!"

Nefaric delivers a devastating blow to my back and I scream in agony. He strikes me with so much force that my body flies into Mach one. My body hits the ground and it creates a major crater in the street. Concrete and dust are in the air and I become trap underneath rubble. My energy is decreasing, and apparent damage is on the Warrior-suit. Doubts start swirling in my psyche and losing faith in my abilities. Maybe, I am over my head. Nefaric is the superior fighter and I can't handle his aggression. This is the Chief of Forces with thousands of years of warfare experience. How can I compete with this? Through the cracks of the rubble, I see Nefaric charging up for another energy beam!

"Ha-ha-ha! Let me see if you can dodge this......HA!"

A hot scarlet beam derives from his hands which is coming directly towards me. The energy is so fiery that I feel the heat before it contacts me. By a divine miracle, I gloved-blast the rubble and avoid the explosion. I start panting for oxygen and every breath I take becomes precious. For a safe escape, I fly on top of skyscraper to regroup myself with my hands on my knees and trying to regain air in my lungs. For moment, I thought I had a break. Unluckily, Nefaric is in my face waiting for my next move.

"Where are you going, Kenji? Had enough?" said Nefaric.

"How did you get here, so fast?" I said with frustration and confusion "You don't have the ions for that level of speed and agility! How is it possible? Did you find my father's blueprints?"

"Zerk and Ollo provided me their services to build this armor. They have engineered speed and agility. Nefaric explains.

"Zerk and Ollo are from Gallium and Radium. Why would they help you?"

"We captured those fugitives in battle, and they became our slaves. We spared their lives for a special engineering project. Zerk and Ollo created a powerful combat armor for the sole purpose to defeat you. It's quite sidesplitting when you instill fear in one soul. Zerk and Ollo compromise their own convictions to survive. On the contrary, an Allonian would have too much pride to forfeit to the enemy. I wouldn't sacrifice my core values for no one. By the way, my suit is swift and sufficient to take advantage of your combat inexperience. Let me show you an impeccable illustration!"

Nefaric uses a roundhouse kick me in the chest me off the building and I splash in the depths of the ocean. I drift onto the ocean floor and a school of fish starts pecking at my Warrior-suit. Nefaric dives in the water in a relentless pursuit to shoot more energy beams at me. He discharges one and I deflect it back. Nefaric dodges it with ease and shoots energy spheres at a rapid pace. I deflect each one and swim to the top of the water. I fly into the skies which creates big waves from the aftereffects. Nefaric swims to the top as well and follows me into the air.

"Who is the coward now? Why are you leaving from battle?" said Nefaric.

Nefaric did not know that I had a strategy. He assumes I am running away like a weakling, but he is falling for the carrot on the string strategy. I fly past the o-zone layer and into outer space. As Nefaric enters the o-zone and gains distance to catch up to me, I take my wings and sword, convert it into the cannon, and discharge a full blast.

"This is for Candor!"

The cannon became extremely hot that I feel a burning sensation on my fingertips as I pull the trigger. It is a direct hit.

"Ahhhhh!" yells Nefaric.

Nefaric plots into the Pacific Ocean which generates a nuclear explosion! The explosion is so massive that astronauts from their space stations could see it without glasses. With caution, I fly back to Earth to make sure that Nefaric is eradicated. For now, I don't see any sign of him. To be more vigilant, I put incognito mode to see if I can pick up his body heat. There is zero sign of Nefaric. Mission is complete.

With a victorious emotion, I fly back to Tokyo and the land on top of the skyscraper. The battles are continuing, and I am ready to assist them. Before I am able to engage in battle a familiar and evil voice is back........ Nefaric!

"Oh my, oh my. I am overly impressed by you Kenji. Now that was a beautiful attack. I must say, that's very Allonian of you. "said Nefaric with a disheveled armor.

"How......how the hell did you survive?" I said in shock.

"Ha-ha! Why are you so puzzled? You should know by now that I will never be defeated or die Kenji. It's simply and utterly impossible. My suit can bear a massive attack with that powerful magnitude. Remember who I am. Nefaric, the Chief of Forces will kill you with or without my armor."

Nefaric is chuckling with confidence but he is conspicuously injured from the blast. There are significant lacerations on his chest and arms. He's arching over and holding his ribs.

"You're bluffing, Nefaric. Your foolish pride is causing you to speak an absurd dialect. You are weak, and I can eliminate your life right now. With my small ounce of empathy and mercy, just surrender and exit my planet. Relinquish the throne to me and I will repair the damage that you cause upon Alloy, Gallium, and Radium. As the new King of Alloy, I hereby banish you from Alloy. You are longer the Chief of Forces. Your duties are relieved. Just do me a great favor for Alloy and disappear with your dishonor. You shall never return."

"I will surrender…. your love."

"Huh? What are you trying to say?"

"After analyzing your brain waves, I know what is dear in your heart. Is her name, Amaya?"

"Wait…. what about her?"

Nefaric gingerly stands up and smirks devilishly.

"I know how much Amaya means to you. She is your love of your life. The brightest star in the cosmos. Your precious treasure."

"Shut the hell up, Nefaric. I am tired of your gratuitous and long-winded speeches. Do not speak about Amaya. I ask you again, surrender the throne and leave my planet at once!"

"Fine, I won't speak about your main squeeze, but I will bring her to existence."

Nefaric lifts his arm and wave his hand towards the ground. Abruptly, a tubular portal appears and summons Amaya! With aggression, Nefaric wraps his arm around her neck with the plasma sword across her neck.

"What are you doing? Let her go!" I plead.

"Give me the medallion or she dies! What's more important, your hollow pride or her?" said Nefaric.

Part of me did not want to sacrifice the medallion, but I don't want Amaya to perish. Compromising with the enemy will compromise my ideals and convictions. However, I am at a rock and hard place between the love of my life and protecting Earth. To spare Amaya's life, I give him a diplomatic offer that puts him in a persuading position.

"If you take her life, I will kill you right afterwards. Taking her life will be counterproductive. Let her go at once. Nefaric, I have the minimum amount of mercy to make a suitable deal in which it can benefit both parties. Nefaric, I will give you the medallion when I return to Alloy however, I must have an intricate role with the Allonian Army. The continual violence must cease, and Alloy must stop the war. Once I arrive at Alloy, I will duplicate a medallion for you that possesses the same capabilities and features. We can restore Alloy to glory and greatness. As per request, please let Amaya go. She has nothing to do with this. As a true Allonian soldier and god, do what is honorable."

Within seconds and without uttering a single word, Nefaric holsters his plasma sword and releases Amaya from his grasp. I begin to take off my mask and Amaya runs into my arms for an empathetic hug.

"Kenji? What are you wearing? What's going on? I am confused and frightened." said Amaya.

"Amaya, I know this may sound farfetched, but I am not what you think I am. I am God from the planet Alloy. There's a lot to explain and I will give you all of the information about my origins, but I have to leave Earth for the restoration my planet. I am the next King of Alloy."

"No, it's not your planet. Alloy doesn't belong to you nor shall you return there. "Amaya said, Nefaric is the king. Your father is a traitor and you must pay his debts."

CHAPTER 12

POWER OF THE HUMAN SPIRIT

"Wait, what!" I said in full disbelief.

Amaya transforms into an Allonian Army uniform and her skin becomes metallic! She roundhouse kicks me in the face and punches my stomach. With uncanny force, she tears my medallion from my chest, and I transform back to my street clothes. I am laying on the ground in full pain, but I am hurting more from Amaya's betrayal.

"Ha, ha, ha! I am always one step ahead of you Kenji. The art of war is painted with many strokes. You are doodling with your fingers while I illustrate a beautiful game plan to defeat you. This is my first lieutenant Flero. She is second in command of the Espionage Brigade. We assigned her to Earth to spy on your movements and location. Kenji, did you fall in love with our spy? Flero is beautiful and lovely, isn't she? 1Lt. Flero is a top-notch soldier that's willing to put the mission first. Her mastery in deception is her greatest attribute and essential asset to our glorious Allonian Army.

Alloy always comes first unlike your disloyal father who put his interests ahead of our planet. Father like son. You were negotiating with the enemy to save a woman? Are you mad? You're willing to sacrifice your entire Earth for your own self-interest? How selfish you are! Rule number one, Kenji. Don't compromise with the enemy. This is a rule that your father broke with the AFOP Act. Allonians will never cooperate with planets Gallium and Radium. There is no such thing as pacifism. Your father had his ludicrous philosophies that were detrimental to Allonians ways of life. This is my time to rule the throne. I must say, you appear to be useless and weak without your armor. You're absolutely nothing without it. Flero, hand over the medallion."

"Yes, my lord. Before I hand over the medallion, may I finish the deed and kill Kenji." said Flero.

"What a fabulous idea! Yes, you may. You can kill him fast or slow. I prefer slow but it's your personal preference."

Flero draws a long purple plasma sword and I am laying on the ground helpless. My body is broken but it's pale in comparison to my heart. I genuinely loved Amaya. She made me feel important and took the time to understand me. I didn't see this coming. How could a loving, nurturing, and wonderful being become a cunning, deceiving, and devilish foe? Flero walks slowly and I am consuming with flowing tears and numbness.

"Amaya, how......how could you? "I said in disbelief.

"My name isn't Amaya, it's Flero. The second cell phone is a data hub for our Allonian Army Command Post. With your data, I was able to track your whereabouts. After I eliminate you, we will make Earth into an afterthought. You were a pleasant guy, Kenji but I must follow orders from my King Nefaric. It is nice acquainting with you Kenji Jackson. Prepare for the next chapter in hell. Get on your knees, now!"

Grudgingly, I get on my knees and anticipate my death. The plasma heat is absurdly hot as she aims her blade to my neck.

"Guillotine style? Impressive. It will be a bloodbath mess but satisfying. Kenji, we could have been a glorious royal family, but you decided to follow your father's footsteps. Now you will end just like him. Oh, the beautiful irony. Flero, finish the deed!"

"Yes, my lord." said Flero

Flero swings her sword but halts midway. Suddenly, Flero shoots a potent beam at Nefaric!

"Ahhh, 1Lt. Flero!" screams Nefaric in pain and drops to his knees.

"Why? What in Alloy's name are you doing!" said Nefaric.

"I am not 1Lt. Flero. I am not Amaya. I am not Allonian. I am Samari, the daughter of Ollo."

"What the hell?" I said. "How many names do you have?"

"Just one name and it's Samari. I am from Gallium and my father Ollo is kidnapped by the Allonians." said Samari. "The planet Alloy must pay for their debts. With my father's reconfiguration technique, I can transform into anything. Nefaric was desperate for military personnel in the Espionage unit and I took advantage of the opportunity to enlist in the Allonian Army. I disguised myself as an Allonian from head to toe and passed their rigorous vetting. By entering the Espionage Brigade, I was able to obtain all the top-secret information. I learned the AFOP Act and here is my true form."

Once again, Samari changes into a different person. It didn't really matter what she changes into because her beauty improves in each of her transformations. This time, her complexion turns into a reddish tone and her hair converts into a long and silky-blue color with blonde streaks. Samari's eyes are purple which resemblances an emerald. Her armor remains intact with a slight color modification of a brighter hue.

"This is my true form. Kenji, I am sincerely sorry to deceive you. Amaya may not be real but my love for you is truly genuine. My initial mission is to confiscate the medallion and assassinating the future king of Alloy. Revenge and retribution crept in my mind while I was on Earth. I know you are not part of the Nefaric's regime Kenji, but you are Allonian. We can't be allies. There's too much bloodshed for peace to exist. With the compassionate in my heart, I will spare your life. Nevertheless, at this specific moment, this destructive medallion will belong to me. The Allonian Army committed heinous crimes over upon my people including killing our King! I must free my father and Gallium from Allonian oppression I shall never forgive a man that commits treacherous acts to my family and the people of Gallium. My planet was once a thriving one please where my people were autonomous, intelligent, and forward thinkers. Gallos are people who love to be free and explore the upper horizons for a healthier galaxy. Now, Gallos are reduced to tyranny and fear with no options."

"Wait, Samari. There's too much misinformation being filtered. The AFOP Act was invented to generate energy for all three planets. Were there mistakes that happened? Yes. Did we fight and lost lives in wars over it? Yes. However, I will be the next King. I want to end the wars and amend the atrocities that occurred. Gallium, Radium, and Alloy lost their kings due to Nefaric. He's the reason there's chaos and unbalance. My father Candor wanted to help every God from each planet to be vigorous and efficient. I mirror my father's values and philosophies. If you take the time and hear my vision, I know with tremendous confidence that your planet Gallium will be restore again. Gods should not fight each other but work together with full cohesion. Gods' purpose is creating life, not destroy it. Samari, please hand me back the medallion. My purpose in life is to restore the three planets and we can regain peace. That medallion is the keystone towards everlasting stability.

Samari, I am not an extension of Nefaric. I am a descendant of my father Candor who wanted to help the world with enhancing technology for the greater good, not oppression or colonization. Earth possesses key elements that are not found on Alloy, Gallium or Radium that can regenerate the ions. With an enhance version of ions, we can restore all three planets. It's here on Earth! Let's research together and create the peace back to the planets. The medallion is too valuable to sabotage."

"Sorry, Kenji. I can't do it. I know your heart is in the right place, but you haven't experience true loss. I experience too much loss in the hands of the Allonian Army. They murdered my people and enslaved the Gallos including my father. There's too much antipathy in my soul to see any optimism for the future. The damage is beyond repair like light escaping a black hole. I apologize Kenji, but this medallion must be destroyed and Nefaric must die."

"Samari, please listen. I will never fathom your pain and suffering but I can only empathize your struggles. We can make things right. I'll return to the throne and end this chaos. The only way this pandemonium will cease is the medallion. You do believe what I am saying?"

"Yes, Kenji. I believe what you're saying is hopeful truth, but I think we are on two different paths. I want to say thank you for being decent and kind. I love you Kenji, you have a heart of gold. You made me feel special and unique. A feeling that I haven't felt before. You are not a typical Allonian. Kenji, I love your optimism and innovative ideas for the planets, but I must help my people now. I can no longer wait for research or something to happen. I must abolish the medallion at once to end the mayhem!"

Samari tosses the medallion in the air and shoots an energy ball towards it. Suddenly, Nefaric flies in Mach speed and obtains the medallion mid-air!

"I wasn't quite dead yet. While you lovebirds were chitchatting, I restored plentiful of energy to heal myself. Now, with the medallion in my grasp, I will become invincible. I waited my whole life for this moment. No God will defeat me now!"

"Give it back, Nefaric!" I yell.

"Ha-ha-ha! Never. Kenji, I gave you a golden opportunity to join the Allonians, but you turn your back on us. It's a pity. Now, it's time for retribution!"

Nefaric activates the medallion and the transformation is awfully powerful. Winds are blowing at 500 miles per hour and I fly off the skyscraper! Samari flies and catches me right before I hit the asphalt. Nefaric's laugh echoes with flamboyancy and wickedness. The transformation ends and there is an eerie silence. Regret and apprehension start to foster in my mind. I should've taken out Nefaric when I had the chance. With no armor, I don't feel like I am able to battle with Nefaric. I ultimately failed Earth, my family, and myself. Suddenly, Nefaric hovers down with authority and lands on the asphalt. He's stronger than ever with the Warrior-suit.

"Oh, my Warrior-suit is incredible." Nefaric said in amazement. "It's amazing, astonishing, and fantastic! I never had this powerful before. I do not need an army with this. So, where is the backstabbing bitch?"

"Hey, don't call her that you prick!" I reply.

"It's alright Kenji, I will fight him. Wait here."

"Samari…"

Samari draws her sword and starts flying towards Nefaric. I begin to worry that she may not be strong enough to battle with Nefaric. Nevertheless, I admire her grit and courage.

"Betrayal and treason results to death according to the penal code of Allonian By-Laws. You shall bleed upon my hands." said Nefaric.

"I rather die with integrity than be a subservient slave." said Samari.

"Your just as pathetic as your father Ollo. As commanded, he will get on his knees and clean my palace for the rest of his valueless life!"

"You are a heartless monster! Die!"

Samari shoots an electrifying and potent beam at Nefaric in which he penetrates multiple skyscrapers. Buildings implode from the force causing a miniature earthquake. There is no sign of Nefaric, and victory seems evitable for a moment.

"Wow, Samari you did it! You defeated Nefaric!" I yell with jubilee.

"The nightmare is officially over. I can return to Gallium in peace. Take care, Kenji. I will miss you dearly. You know how to make a goddess feel like a lady."

"Samari, I can come with you. Let me come fix Gallium and the other planets."

"No, stay here. Your home planet is Earth. My planet is Gallium. I must fight my own battles. Please understand."

Samari caresses my face and gives me a gentle kiss on my lips and flies away to the stratosphere. A small tear walks across my cheek as I see her leaving for Gallium. As Samari drifts into the sunset, Nefaric reappears! He's floating in mid-air with an energy ball that is ready to discharge.

"You thought you slayed me? I am a God of Alloy; you can't eradicate me! I will send you to a permanent vacation to hell!" Nefaric said in full rage.

Nefaric shoots a beam from the glove blasters which directly hits Samari. Samari tumbles into the ocean and drops to the bottom of the sea floor. Numbness overwhelms me in which I become directly despondent.

"You are an animal! "I yell.

"I did what is required. She was a treacherous cretin that deserves to perish with the rest of the rodents. Nephew, I sincerely apologize that I had to kill your significant other. It truly hurts me more than it hurts you. I am also sorry that I must kill you too. The family reunion was quite lovely, and we had some quality uncle and nephew time. I will forever cherish you forever in my memories but it's time for you to go to hell with her. Let's call it, a wonderful honeymoon to your demise."

Nefaric starts powering up with glove blasters. The ground is shaking and the vibrations from the powering up is causing more buildings to collapse. The temperature becomes cold and hot simultaneously which is abnormal. The ocean water is converting into tidal waves. The bridges are swaying like Polynesian palm trees. The Allonian Army and NATO Forces cease their fighting to witness the spectacle. My mind starts racing and my emotions begin to run wilder than the Serengeti. The pain and anguish from repress memories begin to swirl in my psyche and the adrenaline begins to kick in full gear. The recurring memory of the loss of my father and Samari triggers a button a deep state of mind. Nefaric's deplorable actions took me over the emotional cliff and put me into an unsustainable rage that I never experience before. My heart begins to pump harder and a fiery wrath consumes me.

"Hey, Kenji. It was an honor to fight you in battle. You fought like an Allonian. A weak one that deserves to bury like your father. Killing my father and Candor was very satisfying but you will be my ultimate execution. The Nefaric Dynasty will continue for eternity! I can conquer a planet and become the invincible God in all the galaxies. Enjoy your death as I will. Ha-Ha-Ha!"

Nefaric shoots the beam towards me. Time sits still for a moment. Death is coming within a few feet nonetheless; I am not afraid. As the fatal energy beam inches closer to me, I raise my hand and halt the attack. Nefaric is dumbfounded.

"What the......" utters Nefaric.

13: Power of the Human Spirit

An epiphany crosses my cognition. The medallion is made with "organic steel" which means it's a living organism that continuously grows within my body. The ions from the Warrior-suit seeps through my skin which generates a new chemical bounding in which produces a new atom. This atom can only fuse with human DNA and since I have the components of human and god, I am able to produce this new enhanced power. Gods can create many things, but they do not determine outcomes. With the exposure of the Earth's environment and experiences, I can do something that is unlike the Gods which is able to use the human spirit to form into battle armor without a medallion. This may be the missing link that my father has been awaiting from his research. Humans are born with souls. Some humans may untap their souls and some repress this feeling, but the abstract idea of a soul isn't a façade. With a medallion, it produces new atoms which fuses with the energy from the human soul. A strong defense mechanism develops and a potent power manifest. With the combinations of ions, soul, and willpower, it doubles the power that any God will ever obtain. Now, I understand my father's genius works.

As the energy beam halts in mid-air, I transform into my new armor. It's unlike my Warrior-suit because it's my skin that becomes metallic including my hair. Head to toe, I become a bluish-silver being with powers that surpasses the original Warrior-suit. When wearing the Warrior-suit, it felt heavy when it came to lateral movement, but now I feel loose and agile. The adrenaline from my rage continues to produce massive energy and I feel unassailable. With gravitational heave, I redirect the beam towards the skies to avoid severe damage to Tokyo. My focus is supreme, and I tread with poise towards Nefaric. I sense his dismay and fear as I walk closer towards him.

"This is impossible? I have the medallion, how the hell did you possess this war armor?"

"Do not be concern about it. Gaining knowledge about this new suit is irrelevant information to you. I gave you a chance for a partnership and resolution, but I recognize that I will never convince you to partake in any rectification for the three planets. Negativity, destruction, and wretchedness are the only components you care about. You may have a difficult upbringing, but so have I. However, I didn't let pessimism to consume my soul. Adversity made me the God that I am today. Adversity is something you can't manifest. It's something you can't create or buy. Sometimes in life, you must endure pain to experience joy. Taking away one's joy to fulfill a void isn't my philosophy. You thought taking away the joy and lives from Radium, Gallium, and your own family will fulfill that everlasting need of being respected but it does not. You're not hailed, you are feared. You possess an eternal wickedness within your heart. Honestly, I feel compassionate for your poor soul. The anger and envy of Candor blinded your judgement causing the destruction of the Allonian kingdom. Living life of constant chaos engulf you into misery. As the next King of Alloy, it is my duty to eliminate that fear. I will take back the medallion and end your reign as king. No more warnings, no more chances. You are finish, Nefaric."

"Nephew, that was a phenomenal speech. Articulate and well spoken. You caught me off guard with your new fancy outfit but it's time to end this squabble. Try to dodge this attack!"

Nefaric shoots another powerful beam but I halt it once again and redirect it towards the skies.

"How are you doing this? You do not have the medallion. This is preposterous!"

"Something you don't underestimate which is the human spirit. Humans may be weak in stature, but they possess something powerful which is deep inside their anatomy which is their soul. This powerful mechanism helps connects humans even if they are different in complexion or culture. That's something you need to learn but I fear it's too late for you to change. You don't have compassion or remorse. Fear is what fuels your heartless soul. Those who wish upon hatred, destruction and death on others does not deserve to exist on any planet or galaxy. It's time for me to put you in your place. Your anarchistic and narcissism is your ultimate downfall."

"Shut your face! I don't need to be marginalize by an inferior opponent. You want to put me in my place? Draw your sword now!"

From my new untap energy, my plasma sword appears through my palms. The handle on the sword in Allonian hieroglyphics reads "King Kenji" one side and "Candor" on the other. The hue of the plasma is teal which mirrors the Pacific Ocean. The sword is tenacious, fierce, and battle ready.

"As you wish, Nefaric."

Nefaric draws his sword and flies towards me in Mach speed. Swords clash and we fight throughout the city and within air. Every time the swords clank, it replicates a thunderous sound. Nefaric is giving his best and I see his sweat dripping down his face. Multiple buildings crumbles from the sound our battle.

"This doesn't make sense! I am the best swordsman on Alloy! How is an earthling challenging me!"

"I have surpassed you. Accept it. I can end this duel with one more swing. I only humored this fight to see what your limitations are and it's apparent that you are the weaker swordsman. Surrender."

"Never! Over my dead corpse!"

The duel becomes somewhat mind-numbingly tedious. Nefaric is attempting to use every possible strategic sword attack to disrupt my counters but it is futile. This new-found power changes my reaction time. His sword swings are in slow-motion and with every attempt, Nefaric is becoming weaker. No longer I have to guess his next move because I can see his attacks coming before he can strike me. It's equivalent to knowing the answers before the teacher gave out the test. The laser focus I have is superior. In some respects, this duel is highly unfair for Nefaric however, I do not care. Part of me extends the fight for me to humiliate him.

"Give up Nefaric! You need to stop, or I will stop for you." I said directly to Nefaric as we hover in mid-air.

"Never!"

"Fine, I'll end this duel now. I am becoming very bored with your weak attacks. It's pitiful."

"How dare you!"

With one swing, I hit Nefaric's sword and he propels into the water near the bridge.

"Oh no!"

"Game is over. It's time for your reign to end."

"Please, please I beg of you. Don't kill me."

"You killed my father and the love of my life. Why should care anymore!"

"I am sorry for the death of your father. It was strictly for the greater good or what I thought was the greater good. Please understand. I was only trying to help my beloved Alloy. AFOP Act caused major confusion including Gallium and Radium. I was only trying to do what's best for the Allonians. I love my people and sometimes that love blinds my judgement.

Ok, Kenji. You win. I will admit my defeat. I will officially surrender to you. Kenji, you are the new king of Alloy. Your powers can help change the outlook for our people. I will open to your ideas and we can help the three planets to become peaceful once again. I will end my throne to the kingdom effective immediately. Spare my life. I may not bring back your father or Samari to life, but I will be in your debt for eternity. I will do what you say. Please King Kenji, forgive my sins and I will be in your full command. Let me redeem myself."

Nefaric sticks his hand out for a handshake. Part of me is glad that he admits his transgressions but part of me doesn't trust him. With the little compassion that I had, I become the bigger God and extend my hand.

"Thank you for your mercy, nephew!"

Without hesitation, Nefaric uses a deceptive technique and blinds me with bright light from his palm. I become temporarily blind.

"I had one more trick up my sleeve. You are such a gullible fool. Your kindness is very adorable but your Achilles heel. I know I can't beat you one on one and this light trick will only last a few minutes but it's enough time to obliterate this planet. I will utilize the cannon to eradicate this filthy and primitive planet. It's time for your funeral Kenji with your own weapon!"

Nefaric immediately swoops down into the water to retrieve the sword to assemble the cannon. He flies as high in the sky and the cannon is present.

"I always win, even in death. You will never defeat me Kenji. Say goodbye to Earth!"

Nefaric pulls the trigger and the beam from the cannon penetrates the ocean waters in which creates a massive whirlpool. The whirlpool is so strong that the water swallows multiple yachts, boats, and cargo ships. Nefaric's cowardly light blinding attack fades and I regain my vision. Suddenly, I submerge into the waters to prevent a major explosion. The beam is extremely lethal and lead to the genocide of Earth. The beam is moving at a rapid pace and almost reaches the ocean floor. As the beam inches away to contact Earth, I halt the potential dubious attack. Instead of deflecting the energy blast, I absorb it which fuels my powers to full capacity. With full fiery-rage, I surface from the water and ready to finish the madness for Earth.

"It's time to eliminate your existence. I gave you too many chances. This is for my father, Candor. This is for Samari. This is for Earth. You won't escape this time, rot in pieces." I said as I snatch the medallion from his armor.

"This cannot be! Earth should be smithereens! I can't lose my place to the throne. I am a God of Alloy. You don't have to right to do this!"

"You don't have the right to live!"

I extend my arms and hands which a ball of energy forms. With no hesitation, I deliver a deadly energy blast towards the skies to eliminate Nefaric forever. Nefaric can't escape this attack or talk his way out of it. Death is eminent for him and long deserving.

"Noooooooo!" yells Nefaric.

The energy blast carries Nefaric to space and a supernova explosion manifest upon the stars. It's finally over, Nefaric is no longer king of Alloy.

Immediately, I order the Allonian Army to ceasefire towards NATO.

"Nefaric is no longer King! I am the new King of Alloy. Cease your fire at once and return Alloy now!"

All the Allonian soldiers retreat to their spaceships and ascends to space. I ordered the NATO troops to retreat as well.

"The battle is officially over. We won. Thank you for your brave service. Please return to your base."

The NATO Forces cheers with an intense glee of victory and left Tokyo. As I hover in the air, I witness all of the destruction that our wars did to the city of Tokyo. Buildings and skyscrapers are now rubble. Streets are nearly undrivable. Cars are flipped upside down, fire hydrations are spraying all over the city, fires are dancing on every corner, and potholes are the size of craters. There are dead NATO and Allonian soldiers' bodies lying around the city. With my healing capabilities, I restore all soldiers back to life and order them to retreat to their families. There is one life that I need to restore…. Samari.

14: Kenji, the King of Alloy

After restoring the soldiers' lives, I begin the search for Samari's body in the ocean to salvage her life. I found her lifeless underneath a large reef coral. I carry Samari unto my arms and swim to the surface of the water. My first thoughts are to take her to Mount Tenchi to be with my family and revive her in a safe environment.

"Kenji! You are back!" said Mom. "Wait, why are you so shiny? What's going on?"

"What happened? Are we okay?" said Grandpa. "You look like Christmas ornament."

"Yes, everything is okay, but she is not." I said "Sorry, I am in my new armor. I will return back to normal."

I return to my normal state and I gentle put down Samari's body onto the ground.

"Who is this Kenji? She's a different color than a human!" said Mom.

"Long story. She is not human, Mom. She is from a planet called Gallium. Nefaric killed her in battle and I am attempting to restore her life."

I begin to heal her fatal wounds, but nothing happens.

"Come back to life!" I said, "I brought back the NATO and the Allonian Army back to life."

"You can't bring back a Gallium." said Candor. "It's virtually not possible."

"Why not?"

"You can only heal Allonians and humans because it's part of your DNA. If you had the medallion, perhaps that could work."

"This is unfair!"

"Why do you care for her so much?" said Mom.

"This is Amaya!"

"She's an alien?" said Grandpa.

"Yeah, sort of. But I have no time to explain. Wait, she did touch the medallion with her hand. If there's some residue from the medallion, the ions should seep through her armor and bring her back to life."

"You are correct Kenji. You're a smart kid. It's worth a try."

I place the medallion unto Samari's hand and try to rejuvenate the ion particles to revive her. At first, no sign of life. Suddenly, I see air blowing through her nose and movements in her legs.

"She's alive!" yells Mom in excitement and confusion.

"Is this a magic trick?" said Grandpa.

"No, I can do this to anyone."

"I lived a long time Kenji. If I am dead, I am dead. Don't bring me back, ok!" said Grandpa.

"Ok, Grandpa." I said while I roll my eyes.

"Kenji?" whispers Samari.

"Yes, Samari. I am here. I healed you back to life. Are you alright?"

"Yes, Kenji I am fine. How did we get here? Are we dead?"

"No, no. We are in Mount Tenchi. Remember the class field trip? I found my father's spirit here."

"Your father's spirit? I am very out of whack. Wait, what about Nefaric? Is he still alive?"

"No, I defeated Nefaric. The terror is officially over."

"Thank the heavens. I must go to Gallium now."

"We can't. There's still more research on Earth that we must conduct. Before leaving Earth to Gallium, Radium or Alloy, we must find the missing ions to restore all three planets. We can't just leave without a plan. Please listen to me Samari, I may need your help. I promise we will make

Gallium more beautiful than ever before, but we must find that missing link."

"Since you revived my life, I will honor that request. If you can revive me, don't you think you can revive your father?"

"I don't think it's possible." said Candor.

"Dad, I think I can make it work. The medallion itself still has your DNA prints. With this new originated energy that I summoned in battle; I can use it to restore your life "I said.

"Son, I guess it's worth an attempt. Do what you must."

"Put your hand on the medallion, Father."

Candor places his hand on the medallion and a bright light shimmers throughout the cave, A solid being forms instantaneously. A shadow of a man beings shape upon the cave floors. Candor is back to from the dead and is now a living person once again. My mother cries in bliss. Even my grandfather who is a stoic and detached succumb to emotions with overflowing tears rolling from his face. I didn't cry but I became overwhelmed with excitement that consumed my soul. Who am I kidding, I am crying like a baby that my father is back walking on Earth again.

Though my father is back alive, he is longer a God. From my father's fingerprints on the medallion, there were only a few DNA particles to restore him. However, he can only comeback as a solely as a human. Due to how far removed he was from life and not having a present body, I can't return him into a God. The life energy can only transfer into an able body and since he remains were discarded during the attack, I cannot return him to his true from. Samari is able to be one hundred percent restored due to her death being only a few hours where I could salvage her life. Nonetheless, my father reuniting with my mother and rekindling our family is more significant to any measure.

"Son, thank you for bringing me back. Though I am alive, you are the new King of Alloy. It's up to you to restore the planet."

"Father, I will do what I can. I must find the rest of the ions for the medallion. Somehow, I there was only 15% energy for each Gallium and Radium ions. What happened to the rest of its power?"

My father makes a concerned face.

"Son, there is something I must tell you."

"What is it?"

"Take me to the top of the cave."

"Okay?"

I transport my father on top of Mount Tenchi. There is a beautiful sunrise escaping some clouds and decorating the lands of Japan. For the first time in my life, my father looks nervous and very unnerved.

"Dad, what's going on? Is there something wrong?"

"Nothing is wrong but what I did was wrong."

"Huh?"

"Please hold your emotions. This will be very overwhelming information and I don't want you to carry resentment towards me."

"Dad, you're my father and I am your son. I will love you no matter what. However, I am tired of the secrets and mystery. I hope this is the last secret you have in the tank."

"Indeed, it is but it may change your perspective of me."

"Dad, enough with the stalling. Can you please just tell what the heck is going on?"

"Alright, son. You deserve to know. You are my son, but my first son."

"Huh?"

"You are the rightful Alloy to the throne, but you are not alone."

"Why are you being so cryptic? I still don't comprehend. Are there other Allonians on Earth right now?"

"Ok, it's complicated. You were only an infant and barely breathing air on Earth. While I was alive serving the Air Force, I was on an imperative deployment. The mission was in South America, specifically Brazil. It was a humanitarian mission to provide a Brazil supplies, food, and resources after a devastating flood that wrecked the entire country. The Air Force mission was to deliver an enormous amount of resources in Rio De Janerio. Most of the resources were at a military supply point in Puerto Rico. We have an active Air Force Base there and my troops loaded up on our KC-135 aircraft with the supplies. I was the pilot for the KC-135 and ready to help those who couldn't help themselves during a natural disaster. Before taking off to Rio de Janeiro, I met a beautiful Puerto Rican woman named Gisele Brizuela and..."

"Wait a minute, you had an affair! You cheated on Mom?"

"Uh, in human terms yes but in Allonian culture it is normal. But son, don't rush to judgement."

"Dad, no offense and excuse my language but that is bullshit! How could you! You also held back information from the transfer! How deceiving!"

"Son, I told you to halt your emotions. I knew this new information will disturb you, but son please listen to me first before you lash out. This was part of my research to generate new energy for the three planets. At this time, I couldn't figure out how to generate enough ions. However, after your birth, I sensed a resilient energy that was inside you. You held a power that was stronger than my own and it was due to the human DNA mixing with Allonian DNA. Since humans came from our organic steel, there's an element to humans that Gods do not possess which manifest a power that is tremendously uncanny. Son, you were my breakthrough specimen that helped my research. By duplicating a human with God attributes, it will help rejuvenate the planets.

Kenji, you possessed a power which was a force to be reckon with. Due to that power, I thought I could do the same exact experiment but with different ions. Procreation with a human created a unique and astonishing power that did not exist prior. Zerk and Ollo left planet Earth to return to their home planets which left me in a dire situation. Without Zerk and Ollo, the medallion could never reach its full potential. When Zerk and Ollo left Earth, I thought Nefaric would take their lives. Though I had a sufficient number of ions to get return to Alloy, I didn't have enough ions to restore the planets which is the final goal. I had to do something to clone a Gallo and Radilites, with that concept in mind, I can procreate another Gallo and Radilite by extracting the Alloy ions and substituting with the Gallo and Radilite ions. I procreated with Gisele Brizuela but instead of Alloy ions, it was Gallo ions. The procreation was a success. I conducted the same experiment with a female pilot named Captain Charlotte Webster who I met during the mission at Rio de Janeiro. During our deployment, we bonded and had our relations. Kenji, your birth discovered a new form of energy during battle that surpassed my research expectations. If the others can reach that level of power, there's no doubt that you can restore all three planets. Son, I know my narratives comes across as very obtuse, but It was simply an experiment that was advantageous to our Allonian existence."

"So, I am nothing but an experiment? Is that what I am? Do you not have any moral ethics? You had multiple children and didn't let mother know? Were you just a deadbeat father to the others? I am disgusted by you!"

"Son, I know the truth hurts but you need to know because it will be vital to your next mission."

"Next mission?"

"Your next objective will be to complete my mission which is to save Alloy, Gallium and Radium. Technically, the two offspring are not Allonian. The two specimen belongs to planet Gallium and Radium. You are somewhat related to them, but their percentage of their DNA belongs to their home planets. Son, I love you. You're not just an experiment and I love your mother with all my heart. With my home planet dying, I was only trying to figure out some new alternatives to rectify all three planets. Your potent powers came at a surprise to me. I thought if I can create more of you, it will be beneficial to our future. Also, I wanted to use different birth mothers only because too many ions within a human anatomy can be fatal. It was all based-on science, nothing personal. However, you are my first born which makes it personal. Son, you have every right to feel ashamed, angry, and hurt from my transgressions. I broke the moral ethics code to thrive. It was completely wrong, and I want you to forgive me for it. Nonetheless, the two offspring on Earth could possibly be the link to save all three planets. This is vital information, Kenji and it needed to be said. You must understand that I was only trying to help all three planets even if it's unconventional and grotesque experiments. If you want to get the rest of the ion powers for the medallion to restore the planets, you need to find your siblings."

"My siblings, huh? Wow. This is a lot take in, Dad. I don't know how to feel. I can honestly say that I feel numb to the core. My mind is completely blown from my skull. Brothers? I have half-brothers? Anyways, can you please tell me what their names are, so I can identify them?"

"Nicholas Brizuela and Eric Webster. They do not possess the same levels of powers as you. I intentionally separate the powers which makes you can be the leader of the pact. You must come together as one. It's the only way for peace."

"Are they in Brazil and Puerto Rico? That's where I originally found the ions."

"No, they are in New York City. They were both accepted into a prestigious Ivy League school. Nick and Eric are living at the same campus, but they do not know that they are related, or they are Gods. You have to reveal the truth to them and hopefully, they will oblige to our main objective."

Using my social media app "Flash-Gram", I search for Nicholas Brizuela and Eric Webster. These guys look similar to me but with different complexions. Very surreal and eerie. I took a screenshot and saved them into my phone. Brothers from different mothers. I gained my composure and continue discussing a plan.

"I am already accepted to a litany of Ivy League schools, so I will enroll there. I need further ion energy to save the Alloy Kingdom. Father, I am still somewhat shocked from all of this, but I will only forgive due to the fact you were desperate for a solution. However, this complicates things between you and me. It may take some time to amend this over. You are placing a heavy burden upon my shoulders. Please, no more secrets. That's my only request from this point on. I don't think I can digest another one again."

"Son, I love you and I understand you're hurt. I maybe a God, but I am not perfect."

"Technically, you're a human. For a God, you make too many errors. From this point on, just take care of Mom. I don't think she needs to know this new truth quite yet. Be the husband that she deserves. Mom endured through hell these past few years and I don't want to reveal her something that could sabotage her good spirits. How good is truth if it does more harm than good? I will travel to America and find Nick and Eric. I will reunite the Gods to finish our mission."

"Son, you are a better man and God than I could ever imagine. You're wise beyond your years. Promise me this Kenji. Don't be like me. As a father, I failed you. You shouldn't be in these compromising positions. However, you possess the authority to be more superior than me and the Allonian Kings from the past. You will be King Kenji, the greatest son of Alloy. As I repeat, don't be like me. Be more."

My father puts his hand on my shoulder and gives me a reassuring look in my eyes of redemption. We didn't speak after that moment, but we understood each other.

Be more. Those words resonate because I am more. I am not longer that awkward kid from Jen High but a God from royalty with a great obligation to serve my Alloy people. I am not an only child but a brother to a legacy of powerful beings that does not know their own hidden attributes. I have only scratched the surface. Kenji Jackson, the human is no longer applicable. I am ready to enter the new era as King Kenji, the Galactic Steel God.

David Isaiah Brown was born at Mount Holly, New Jersey but grew up in majority of his adolescents in at Pennsauken, New Jersey. He is a military brat with a Puerto Rican mother, and African-American father who is a retired Chief Master Sergeant in the Air Force. During high school, David Isaiah Brown participated in the school newspaper as a sports writer and football team where he played linebacker. His teachers told him that he was not college material and should take up a trade. Instead of being discouraged, David I. Brown joined the Air Force where he served under three presidents and overseas such as Germany, Qatar, Belgium, England, Netherlands, and Luxembourg. He also participated in the natural disaster for during Hurricane Sandy helping New Jersey civilians to safety.

During his military career, David I. Brown went to enhance his education at Burlington County College and earned his Associate's Degree. He also earned an additional Associate's Degree from Community College of the Air Force. After finishing community college, David I. Brown was accepted to Rutgers University and earned his Bachelor's Degree. David I. Brown is also a member of the Alpha Phi Delta fraternity. He also furthered his education and attended Thomas Edison State University to earn his Master's Degree. Recently, David I. Brown was accepted to Dayton University for his doctorate degree.

David I. Brown is a sports enthusiast. He loves football, basketball, baseball and soccer. He once wrote for the Burlington County Times covering variety of sports. Writing is David I. Brown's passions and he enjoys writing about a plethora of realms such as sports to science fiction. David I. Brown is married to his lovely wife Denika Brown that has two dogs named Cookie and Dude.

Printed in the United States
By Bookmasters